RETRIBUTION

THE HARRY STARKE NOVELS BOOK 7

BLAIR HOWARD

RETRIBUTION

Retribution - Harry Starke Book 7

"I'm a fighter. I believe in the eye-for-an-eye business. I'm no cheek turner. I got no respect for a man who won't hit back. You kill my dog, you better hide your cat." Muhammad Ali

They say revenge is a dish best served cold, and maybe it is, but Harry Starke is already one cold son of a bitch, and when someone brutally murders his kid brother and throws the body into the Tennessee River, that someone had indeed better hide his cat, and do it quickly.

Copyright © 2016 Blair Howard

All rights reserved. No part of this publication may be reproduced, stored in a retrieval system, or transmitted in any form, or by any means, electronic, mechanical, photocopying, recording, or otherwise, without the express written permission of the publisher except for the use of brief quotations in a book review.

Retribution is a work of fiction. The persons, events, buildings and places, depicted in this novel are either the product of the author's imagination or are used fictitiously; no resemblance to actual persons is intended.

Product names, brands, and other trademarks referred to within this book are the property of the respective trademark holders. Unless otherwise specified, no association between the author and any trademark holder is expressed or implied. Nor does the use of such trademarks indicate an endorsement of the products, trademarks, or trademark holders unless so stated. Use of a term in this book should not be regarded as affecting the validity of any trademark, registered trademark, or service mark.

ISBN-13: 978-1536957457

ISBN-10: 1536957453

❀ Created with Vellum

DEDICATION

This one is for my wife, Jo. She has to put up with a lot when I'm writing these novels. Thanks, Jo. I love you.

1

Saturday Evening

He came to slowly, as if waking from a dream. Pain began to course through his body, slowly at first and then with greater intensity, until he was trembling from head to toe. His eyes wouldn't focus, his lips felt glued together, and then he realized that this was no dream—it wasn't even a nightmare. It was for real.

He looked around, but saw nothing. The darkness was total, not a glimmer of light anywhere, and it was quiet, cold, and damp. Cold and damp? But he was sweating. He tried to move and couldn't. He could move his head, and he could breathe, but that was about all. When he did try to move, spears of agony surged upward from his ankles and wrists, and he realized he was tied to a chair—and tied tightly.

He sat still, head back, eyes closed, and breathed

deeply. It helped a little, but the pain.... His *feet* were numb. He tried to wriggle his toes and almost passed out again, the pain was so intense. He stilled his efforts, and waited; the pain subsided into numbness again. He breathed slowly. *Where the hell am I? What happened? Who the f....*

His head throbbed. His mind was a whiteout. Nothing. And then the memories came flooding back.

He remembered going to make the buy. It had been late. Saturday. *But what the hell day is it now?*

He'd been alone, in his car on McCallie. Midnight was just a few ticks of the clock away. The street had been quiet when he pulled around the back of the small, Italianesque strip mall, an incongruous building as out of place on that section of McCallie as a Christian monastery in Raqqa, Iraq. Except for a single black Chevy Tahoe parked close to the steel door at the rear of the building, the parking lot was deserted.

He wasn't concerned. He'd called earlier, talked to Shady, and placed an order. The SUV was exactly where he'd been told it would be. He pulled alongside it, driver's side to driver's side, and rolled down his window. The windows of the other vehicle were heavily tinted, and he couldn't see who was inside, but he still wasn't worried. He waited. Most of the parking lot was in shadows. Not much was visible. After a minute or so he leaned out the window and tapped gently on the window of the other car. The window rolled slowly down, revealing a large, grinning black face surrounded by a nest of thick dreadlocks that reminded him of a bunch of hand-rolled cigars.

"Wha' fo' you wan', mon?" The accent was unmistakably Jamaican.

"You've got something for me, right?"

"What do I got?"

He didn't know what to say to that, and there was a brief, awkward silence. "Okay, that's fine. Never mind. Sorry I bothered you."

He reached for the gearshift, but before he could engage it the grinning face said, "Now wha' fo' you wan' go runnin' off?"

He put the car in gear. "It's no biggy. I made a mistake is all."

"You sure did, Hank." The accent was gone.

He jerked his head around to stare at the man—*How the hell does he know my name?*—and found himself looking down the barrel of the biggest revolver he'd ever seen. It was funny what went through a man's mind in a crisis. All he could think was: *Colt Python.*

"Put your hands on the wheel and sit still. Just do as you're told, and everything will be fine."

So he did as he was told. *What the hell is going on? He's definitely not police.* And the man wasn't who he was supposed to be meeting, either.

Two men got out of the other side of the Chevy, walked around the back, and then up between the two cars to his driver's door. The leading man shoved a gun in through his window, and the Chevy reversed ten feet or so to allow him room to open his door.

"Get yo' ass outa du vee-hi-cul," the taller of the two

men growled, jabbing the gun in his face. "An' take it nice an' easy. You heah?"

Again he did as he was told. He pushed the door open gently, keeping his hands in sight, and then stepped down with them held high.

The smaller of the two men stepped forward and slammed the door shut.

"Turn around, asshole." The man's voice was so high-pitched it almost sounded like a woman's.

Reluctantly, he turned.

There was a blinding flash of white light, and then only blackness until he came to, God only knew where.

He was cold, very cold.

"*Hey!*" He yelled it at the top of his lungs and immediately wished he hadn't. The effort pulled his wrists and ankles against the restraints, and the pain.... He'd never known such agony before.

Once the pain had receded a little he sat quietly, assessing his situation. It wasn't good. *Not good? It's— it's... really, really bad. It's I'm-gonna-friggin'-die bad, is what it is.*

The enormity of it closed in around him like a soggy blanket, and he shivered violently.

As afraid as he was, he eventually dozed off. He was jerked back to reality by the squeal of metal scraping against metal—rusty, worn-out hinges. A door opened somewhere above him, and a stream of white light shone down, searing his eyes. He screwed them shut and lowered his chin to his chest. And then the lights came on. He could see now, but barely. The room was huge—at least eighty feet by a couple of hundred—and he was dead in the center of it.

Damn, I hope that ain't prophetic.

The light, if it could be called that—shone dimly down from a half dozen incandescent bulbs almost fifty feet above his head. In every direction, the room eventually disappeared into shadows. Three men came through the door and stood on a catwalk that fronted a string of small, prefabricated offices, that hung like nesting boxes the entire width of the room.

"Hey, Hank," the man with dreads shouted down, "you awake yet?"

Hank squinted up, his head to one side in an attempt to avoid the light. Weak as it was, it hurt his eyes.

"I see that you are," the man said lightly, his voice echoing, and after a moment he started down the steps, his two henchmen following. The voice and accent were Southern, but there was no hint of Ebonics, no street slang. It was almost refined, but not quite. The man was black, solidly built, and smartly dressed: well-cut designer jeans, blue and white–checkered shirt, shoes.... He couldn't see them, and he sure as hell didn't care.

Dreads stopped a few feet in front of him, his feet wide apart, hands on his hips. He smiled.

"You know who I am, boy?"

"Er... no, sir."

"I'm Lester Tree. Your worst nightmare. And I want my money."

"Shady? Shady Tree? Money? What money? I always pay for the score."

"Not the pookie, you moron. You owe me almost fourteen large and I want—"

Before he could finish, the smaller of Tree's two honchoes stepped forward and slapped Hank's face so hard he thought his teeth had come loose.

"It's *Mr.* Tree to you, butt wipe."

"Now, now Henry.... Hah, you two have the same name. How cool is that? Now, Henry, we don't need none of that violence. Do we Hank? Now where was I? Oh yeah—I want it *now!*"

Hank, his cheek still stinging, looked wildly around. "Oh jeez, you mean Nestor. Look, I didn't know. I don't—I don't have that kind of money. I don't, but I—I... I can get it."

Tree heaved a sigh; the two cronies grinned at one another.

Tree was, like his namesake, a tall man, a black Hulk Hogan. Looking up at him, Hank had a hard time believing the wild tales he'd heard about him. He looked more banker than drug lord; even the dreads were neat and clean.

"Somehow I had an idea you'd say that," Tree said, staring up at the faraway ceiling—it was almost like he was talking to himself.

"Son," he continued, "we have a problem, and it's not just the money, it's a matter of trust and respect, too. See, when you play Texas Hold'em, you're supposed to play with money. Your *own* money. When you run out of your *own* money, you're supposed to get up, leave, and come back another day with more of your *own* money. But that wasn't what you did now was it, Hank? They do call you Hank, right, Henry? Whatever. No, you didn't do that. You wrote notes to Nestor totaling $13,750, which he was good enough to accept. He trusted you, Hank. The money? You lost it, which was to be expected; you played like a total dickhead. And then what did you do, Hank?"

He waited for an answer. He didn't get one.

"I'll tell you what you did. You upped and left like a damn cock-a-roach is what you did, and nobody's seen your ass since. You stiffed Nestor of his fourteen large—which, by default, means you stiffed me. Not a smart thing to do, was it boys?"

Both cronies grinned and shook their heads enthusiastically, in unison.

"I'll get it. I'll get it. I'll get it for you tomorrow. I promise, Shady... Mr. Tree." He corrected himself just in time; the small man had taken a step forward, but Tree raised an arm and stopped him.

"Easy, Henry. Take it easy. You'll get your turn in a minute."

Hank's blood ran cold; he shivered violently; it was that awful feeling that someone had just driven a truck over his grave.

"Oh don't worry, Hank. I'm not gonna to let them hurt you... well, not much. See, I *do* have to teach you a lesson. If I don't, well, you understand, right? I let you off, they'll all think I'm soft. Can't have that now can I? *Cause I ain't!*"

Again he waited for an answer, but Hank said nothing.

"So where will you get my money from, and when?" Tree asked.

"Tomorrow. I promise. From my brother. He'll give it to me. He will. He will."

"Yeah, knowing your brother, I do think he will. Well, he'd better." Tree stared down at him for a few long seconds, then gestured at the two men. "Duvon, Henry, teach this young fella a little lesson. Not too rough... oh hell, I don't have to tell you boys how to handle your business. Just get on with it. I'll be back directly."

Duvon James and Henry Gold were a rare couple. Duvon, dressed in jeans, a black tee, and what could only be called a coat of many colors, was a big man. Not *tall* big, maybe five eleven, but with a solid build and a shock of jet black hair cut short, almost to the scalp. He cut an imposing and scary figure. And Hank was indeed scared.

Duvon's partner, Henry, was an equally rare bird. For some reason he was affecting a sort of 1940s gangster look, and wore a zoot suit in a weird, dark gold color. It had to have been tailored to fit, for Henry Gold was maybe five foot six and 140 pounds sopping wet.

"How you doin', sunshine?" Gold asked pleasantly. He received no answer, and for that Hank was rewarded with a vicious slap across the face.

"I said," he repeated, "how you doin'?

"I'm... okay," Hank said breathlessly, anxious to avoid another teeth-rattling slap.

"That's better. Now den, when we talks to you, you answer. Got it?"

Hank nodded, and received another face-numbing slap.

"That's no answer, bro."

"Yes, yes, yes! Please don't hit me again."

"Oney if you don' do as yous told. Now den, Duvon. You got anythin' to ask our frien'?"

Duvon growled something that even Gold couldn't have understood. Needless to say, Henry couldn't answer, and so Duvon proceeded to beat the living crap out of him. He lost count of how many times he was punched in the face before Gold was able to drag Duvon off. Duvon stepped reluctantly back, half turned, then turned back once more to face Hank.

Hank peered blearily up at him, but the fact that he saw what was coming didn't make it any better.

Duvon pushed Gold aside and landed a haymaker right cross on Hank's jaw. He must have put all of his considerable weight behind it, because Hank heard the loud *snap*, like a tree branch breaking, and then nothing, not even darkness.

"Whada hell you do dat fo'? Gold shrieked at Duvon. "You done killed his ass."

Duvon just stood, still as a pole, his hands still curled into fists but now hanging loosely at his sides, and he looked down at his victim, a twisted smile on his face. He didn't say a word.

"Hey," Shady Tree said loudly as he descended the stairs. "You teach that boy a lesson yet?"

"Oh he done that all right," Gold said quietly. "He done taught him one he'll never forget."

"Well, wake him up. We need to get him outa here. Wait, what the hell? What's wrong with him?"

"Er... Duvon killed his ass."

Tree was obviously horrified. He stared down at the corpse and sucked his lower lip so far into his mouth he almost swallowed it.

"Holy shit.... Do you have any idea what you did? Do you have any idea who he was?"

Gold stared at him, not comprehending.

"I think you just opened the gates of Hades and released the damn Kraken."

2

Monday morning

I woke up that Monday morning feeling better than I had in a long time. I'd had a good week previously, an even better weekend, and thanks to Amanda the renovations to the house were finally finished. She'd put in almost six months of hard work, not just physically but dealing with contractors, designers, and everything else that needed to be done to drag the old pile into the twenty-first century, and she'd done a fantastic job. The house looked brand new, as did the beautifully landscaped gardens that sloped down the east side of Lookout Mountain; the place was fit to be profiled in any one of the fancy magazines she'd spread over every flat space in the house.

The pool? It was a thing of beauty. She'd turned the dilapidated concrete hole in the ground and the thick layer of green slime at the bottom into one of those infinity deals, a sparkling, crystalline body of water that appeared to drop off the edge of the mountain. The view beyond it was spectacular. The entire city was spread out like a jeweled tapestry more than two thousand feet below, and at night it was a constellation of colored lights. That view was one of God's finest gifts, and I was truly thankful.

I said the weekend had been perfect, and I meant it. We'd spent all day Saturday relaxing at home, making good use of the pool and just... well, just taking it easy, which is a rare thing for me.

Most of Sunday we'd spent at the club. In the morning I played eighteen holes with my father and his buddies Judge Strange and ADA Laurence "Larry" Spruce. It was a weekly thing. A good time was had by all, and the round finished with me owing my father, August, the princely sum of twenty-five dollars, which pleased him more than if he'd won the lottery. He always wins with the utmost grace. If you know him, you know that, because he makes no secret of it. Sarcasm? Of course.

"That's twenty-five you owe me, son. You can buy lunch."

Lunch? I thought he was kidding. Hell, I'd only lost $25. Lunch for four, along with drinks, would set me back maybe a couple of hundred bucks... but I agreed. I'd had fun, and I love my old man dearly.

We sat down to eat at around twelve thirty. We'd gotten in off the course about an hour earlier, but the old man insisted on several rounds of drinks—he does love that Bombay Sapphire—and some schmoozing among the movers and shakers that inhabited the lounge at any given hour on any given day, and no wonder; he was one of them himself.

I'm sure you've heard of him. August Starke? You only have to watch the local news to know my father is one of nation's foremost tort lawyers. No, he's not a billionaire, but he's close. His winnings for his clients over the last several years were more than $1.5 billion. He loves those deep pockets. But enough about that.

He was sailing a little close to the wind when we finally joined the ladies at our favorite table, the one in the big bay window overlooking the ninth green.

We ordered food and more drinks—and I thanked God Amanda was driving. She's the love of my life and a treasure, and one of these days I'll make an honest woman of her, sooner rather than later, if she has her way. Nah, it's getting to be that time anyway. I'd already proposed to her, on a crazy trip to Maine from which she returned a millionaire many times over.... Oh no, no. Don't even think that. It's not about the money. As much as she's worth, I'm worth a whole lot more. No, it was the right place and the right time, and I was in the right mood, so I asked her, and she accepted. I turned forty-five this year; she's ten years younger than me, but the clock is ticking.

She turned in her notice at Chanel 7 as soon we got back from Maine. I'd wondered at the time if she was doing the right thing, and I asked her as much. She insisted that she was. That thing with Bob Ryan, my senior investigator, getting shot and almost dying had hit her hard. She was wealthy now, she said, and didn't need to work. So she quit.

She also terminated the lease on her apartment and moved in with me.

"So I can work on the house," was the reason she gave, and she did.

Life was good for me for sure. For her? Well, I hoped so. She certainly wasn't complaining.

And so I'd been working on it for the past several weeks—the future, not the house—without her knowing, and right then, as I sat with my family eating lunch on a perfect Sunday afternoon, I was wondering if I was going to regret not having discussed things with her. Well, whatever would be would be. I really wanted to do something special for her, and, well....

Lunch came, and was eaten with some relish—they do a fine rack of lamb—and then dessert and finally coffee. It was then that Rose, my stepmother, turned the conversation inevitably to... you guessed it, Amanda and me, and when we were tying the knot.

Rose is an absolute darling. Twenty years younger than my dad—that's just three years older than me—she's an incredibly beautiful woman: tall, blonde, perfect skin, perfect figure. When they married there was a lot of talk around the club that she was little more than my old man's trophy wife, that she married him for his money. Not true. She loves him dearly, and I love her for it.

Anyway, as I said, Rose managed to turn the conversation to the highly anticipated—yes, even by me—happy day.

"Harry," Rose said. "It's time you two made up your minds. I can't wait any longer, and I'm sure Amanda can't either. Have you two decided when? I need to know, damn it. There are arrangements to make, clothes to buy, especially clothes to buy—winter, spring or summer—and August can't just drop everything, as you well know—"

"The hell I can't," he interrupted. "I can do as I damn well please. There's nothing that can't be put on hold for a few days. But she's right, son. When, for Christ's sake?"

Oh hell, here we go.

I looked sideways at Amanda. She tilted her head and looked at me with wide eyes. *Yes*, that look said. *When?*

I took a deep breath, leaned back in my seat, stared up at the ceiling, closed my eyes, and said, "How about November twelve, Calypso Key, the Virgin Islands?"

The two squeals I got in answer, from Amanda and Rose, turned every head in the room our way.

"You son of a bitch, Harry Starke," Amanda said, punching my arm with enough force to almost knock me out of my seat. "How long have you been planning that, and why have you not mentioned it to me? I've a good mind to tell you to go to hell."

I gave her the biggest, toothiest grin I could force across my face, and then said, "Go on then."

"Like hell I will," she said, and jumped out of her chair, wrapped her arms around my neck, and laid a kiss on me that should have been reserved only for the bedroom. Needless to say, the dining room erupted in applause.

She finally let go of me and practically fell back into her chair. And then it was Rose's turn, and the kiss she gave me was every bit as amazing as the one Amanda had just laid on me. *Okay, I know what you're thinking, but come on; she's my stepmother for God's sake.*

"So when did you start planning all this?" August asked.

"I dunno really. A week after we got back from Maine, I suppose. You know me. I love the Islands. I'm going to go live out there one of these days. I saw something on one of those TV travel shows about Calypso Key... and, well... it looked right. So I made a few calls and I booked us four four-bedroom villas...."

"*Oh* you big *oaf.*" Amanda punched me again. "What about me? Don't I get any say in all of this? I'm not going." She stuck out her bottom lip, but then she took it back, got up from her chair, leaned over, kissed me gently, and said, "Thank you, my love."

And the conversation continued in like manner on into the afternoon. My plan, by all accounts, was a resounding success. By five o'clock Amanda and I were back on the mountain and in the pool, leaning side by side against the infinity wall, gazing down on the city. Yeah, life was indeed good.

So that was the weekend. Now it was Monday morning, and I was out of bed and ready for the day by 5:15 a.m.

These days, since I moved up here, I look forward to

each new day. I usually get up around five and head out for a two-mile run along the roads on top of the mountain. The air is always fresh and invigorating, and even when the weather is hot, it's always ten degrees cooler up there than it is down in the city.

Sometimes Amanda joins me, sometimes not. That day she decided to get her exercise doing laps in the pool. That being so, I knew I had to get out of the house before she got out of bed. If I didn't, I'd end up in the pool with her. Nice? Yeah, but not a good way to begin the day, or the week for that matter. Time in the pool seems to linger....

Unfortunately, the run took only about fifteen minutes, so I ended up in the pool anyway. By six thirty, though, we were both showered and dressed; she for a day out shopping for wedding goodies, me for a day in the office and all of the drudgery that goes with it. One of these days I'd just turn the whole damned mess over to Bob and let him handle it. *Now there's a thought....*

I arrived at the office around eight thirty as usual and was also, as usual, the last to arrive. Jacque, my PA, was already busy organizing the week's tasks for all the members of the team. Bob, now fully recovered from his horrendous wound at the hands of one of Conrad Rösche's security guards, had moved himself into the cubicle of an office next to mine. Tim... well, Tim, now surrounded by more fancy equipment than NASA's Mission Control, was already lost in a world known only to himself.

At the end of our usual Monday morning staff

meeting in the conference room, I took a deep breath, stood, and looked around the small group that had been my world for almost ten years.

"Okay, my fine and gifted crew," I began. "I have an announcement to make." And then I stopped, not quite sure where I was going with it.

"You think we don't know, you ass?" Bob said, leaning back in his chair, his hands behind his head.

"Congratulations, boss!" They said it all in unison, and all I could do was stand there grinning like a moron.

"Jeez, does nothing get past you guys? How did you know?"

"You bin actin' goofy for more than a mont'," Jacque said, smiling. "What else could it be?" Her Jamaican accent, rarely ever present, was as heavy as I'd ever heard it. She came around the table, wrapped her arms around me, and squeezed.

"When will you be doin' it Harry?" I think that must have been only the third or fourth time she'd ever called me by my first name, not that I'd forbidden it; it was out of respect for me as her boss, I suppose.

"November twelve. You're all coming. Every last one of you, and your significant others. We'll wrap things up here on the afternoon of the tenth, shelve what can't be wrapped, and close this place down. You'll all receive full pay for the time off. We're going to Calypso Key in the Virgin Islands for a couple of weeks. Amanda and I will tie the knot on the beach, on the twelfth, and then we'll all spend the next two weeks eating like pigs and drinking like fish, sailing, swimming, scuba diving, or just plain lounging around. I need a rest and you guys do too, and you deserve one, and you're going to get it. And...." I paused for effect. "Everyone gets a five-thousand-dollar bonus before we leave—and no, the trip will cost you nothing; the five grand is my wedding gift to you, and a token of my appreciation for all you've done for me and this company for the last God knows how long.... I love you all." And with that, I turned and walked quickly from the room and into my office, leaving them in stunned silence.

So it was a good start to the week, but my good mood ended no more than thirty minutes later with a phone call from Doc Sheddon, the local Medical Examiner.

"Harry," he said, "I just got off the phone with your dad, and I'd tell you congratulations, but... in all conscience, I can't, at least not now. I need you come to my office. Right now."

I would have asked him why, but before I could, he hung up, leaving me staring vacantly at the handset. Slowly, gently, I returned it to its cradle.

What the hell...? What, the, hell?

3

Monday - Late Morning

It's usually a fifteen-minute drive from my offices on Georgia to the forensic center where Doc Sheddon holds court, but that day I made it in ten. All the way there my mind was in a whirl. What the hell was going on? I'd had dozens of calls from Sheddon, but never one like that. He always, *always* told me what was going on and why he needed me. More to the point, the man had never hung up on me in his life.

I parked the Maxima out back and went in through the rear entrance to the waiting area—it was frigging crowded, and when I saw that, I knew something was terribly wrong.

The first thing I remember as I walked in was Rose taking a flying leap at me; she was sobbing as she flung her arms around my neck. The next thing I saw was my father, seated in an easy chair, his elbows on his knees, head in his hands. And that wasn't all. Kate Gazzara was there too, and she had a look on her face like none I'd ever seen before—something between shock and grief.

Christ, what the hell is going on?

I untangled myself from Rose just as Amanda came through the front door.

She spotted me, grabbed me, arms tight around my neck, and whispered in my ear, "Oh my God, Harry, I'm so sorry."

I pushed her away. I was totally baffled.

"What? What the hell's happened? Where's Sheddon?"

She looked up at me, tears in her eyes. "You don't know? It's Henry. He's dead, Harry."

I had my hands locked onto her upper arms, holding her away from me. For a few seconds it didn't sink in, and then I let her go, my arms dropped to my sides, and I began backing away from her, shaking my head.

"Sit down, Harry," Sheddon said. He was standing in the doorway, hands in his pockets. His voice was very gentle.

So I sat. I looked at him, then at Amanda, then Kate, then at my father—he was shaking from head to toe—then at Rose, who was still weeping.

"Take a minute," Sheddon said, "Then we'll talk."

I jumped to my feet, "I want to see him, now."

"No, Harry...."

I shoved Sheddon aside and almost ran to the autopsy

room. I flung the doors open... and there he was, my kid brother, Henry—or Hank, as he liked to be called—lying on the stainless steel table, still clothed, and soaking wet.

I must have walked to the table, but I don't remember doing it. One second I was standing in the doorway; the next I was by his side. His face was the color of rotten fish, but it was the damage to it that caused me to suck in my breath. It looked like he'd been through the weir gates of Nickajack Dam. There wasn't an inch that wasn't cut, busted, or bruised. Someone had done a number on him.

Holy Mary Mother of God....

No, I'm not Catholic, but that was the thought that came into my head.

"Come on, Harry. Let's get you out of here," Sheddon said. He put a hand on my arm, but I shrugged it away, shaking my head.

"What happened to him."

"Not here, Harry. Let's go to my office."

"No, Doc. Here. I want to hear it while I'm with him."

Sheddon sighed, shook his head, then sighed again and said, "We don't know. Not yet. I'll need to do the post, before—"

"I'll be here for that."

"Harry.... Remember when it was Chief Johnston's daughter in here, and you said—"

"Don't say it, Richard," That was a first, and I could tell it shocked him. No one ever called him by his first name. "So tell me," I said.

"Jeez. Alright. Well, Tennessee Wildlife found him at 10:15 this morning in the river on the south shore, just west of the coastguard station. I was called out, of course, and as soon as I saw him I knew who he was. He was within the city limits, so I called Kate. She'll take the lead in the investigation. Couldn't leave it to anyone else, could we? Then I called your dad and... well. My God, Harry, come on. You can't stay in here, and I can't let you attend the post. You know that."

"I'll be here," I said, quietly. "When?"

"Christ," he whispered. "This afternoon, early; one o'clock. Go see to your folks, Harry. They need you, and I need you out of here."

"I'll see you at 12:45," I told him, and left him standing there beside my brother.

Henry was just twenty-six years old, nineteen years younger than me. My mother died of breast cancer back in '86 when I was fifteen. Dad married Rose three years later, and Henry was born a year after that. He was Rose's only child; he was my only sibling. We hadn't seen a whole lot of each other over the years after he grew up— when he was a kid, yes—but we loved each other. He knew that, and I knew it too.

Dad did the right thing by him, as he'd done by me: Henry attended McCallie, same as I had, and then Washington and Lee. But Henry was more like his mother, a soft and lovable kid. I'd taken after our old man.

And all was well until maybe three years ago. He graduated college in 2013 and then... well, the way he told it he met the love of his life. And the love of his life turned out to be a real piece of work. She introduced him to the finer things in life: fine weed, fine cocaine, fine heroin, and all the other wonderful things that went with them.

No, I wasn't really surprised he'd ended up on a table in Doc Sheddon's little house of horrors, but I was utterly devastated by it. I loved that goofy kid—much more than I'd thought I had. And as I turned to rejoin my family, there was a turbulent river of emotions in me the likes of which I'd never felt before.

There's no way to explain how I felt that day. Oh yeah, I was angry, white-hot, raging. Every muscle in my body seemed to be cramping. My throat was dry, my head was... blank, dead space, a white whirling chasm of nothing but pain and—and horror. But mostly I was inundated by an overwhelming sadness. Time seemed to stand still. I moved like an automaton, and like before, one second I was standing there beside the table, the next I was pushing through autopsy room doors; then I was on my knees in front of Rose and my father. We had our arms tight around each other and all three of us were sobbing. Somewhere in the background I could hear Amanda sniffling.

It must have been an hour later when I called Jacque and told her what had happened, and that I wouldn't be back into the office until... well, I didn't know when. I asked her to tell the others. That was more out of respect than anything else. I wanted them to hear it from me—indirectly, anyway—not from the news.

Monday, September 19, 2016, a day that had begun with great promise, had turned into a nightmare. It was a day I'd never forget. A day that turned me into... a monster.

4

Monday Afternoon, Late

Henry's postmortem was, as all posts are for those who don't see them done on a semi-daily basis, a horror. On the best of days, a postmortem is an experience of utter despair. When it's a loved one that's under the knife, it's... it's the total violation, degradation, and humiliation of what had once been a very special human being.

As I watched Doc carve up my brother, I had flashback after flashback to happier times, some long gone, some not so much. I saw him in Rose's arms, barely hours old. saw myself playing with him as a toddler. Picking him up from kindergarten, driving him around the golf course on a cart. And then there were his birthdays. With each one he grew in size, but he never really did grow up. I'd attended his high school football games, and I'd attended his graduation from McCallie and from Washington and Lee. And you know what? Never in all those years had I seen that boy angry. Never a disparaging or angry word did he utter. He was gentle, kind, and caring, even when he was stoned.

And so I stood quietly by as Doc Sheddon literally took my kid brother apart. Kate stood stoically by my side. That she didn't approve of my being there was obvious to one and all, but the hell with them, and her too.

Doc? Usually his approach to an autopsy is a lighthearted one, the product of many years dealing with the dead and trying to figure out what happened to them. His banter during the work was sometimes humorous—gallows humor—but never did he disrespect his "clients." His attitude was that he was the only voice these people had to tell their story, and tell it he would. Many a killer was doing "all day and a night" in prison because Doc's patients put them there. That day, however, he was subdued. There was no banter, just the drone of his voice for the recorder as he worked his way through the procedure.

"Ligature marks at the ankles and wrists. The victim was restrained, probably with electrical ties.... Severe bruising to the chest, face, jaw, and neck.... Fracture of the fourth cervical vertebrae...."

I'm not going to go into any more of the details. You don't want to know. Hell, I didn't want to know, but I had to. What I will tell you is that when that autopsy was finished, I was a changed man, and not for the better.

Amanda was waiting for us when we came out, and

she joined us in Doc's office, where he poured himself a coffee. Nobody else took him up on his offer.

It was quiet. I think no one wanted be the one to speak first. I grew more frustrated by the minute, and finally Doc sighed and began.

"Well, we knew before we began that this was a homicide. There was no water in his lungs, so he didn't drown. He died of a broken neck caused by a heavy blow to the left side of his jaw. The blow was so severe that the mandible—the jaw bone—was shattered, broken in three places. The left zygomatic, or malar bone—the cheekbone—was also broken, also by a heavy blow, probably the same blow that broke his neck. He was beaten to death, and it wasn't quick. He probably didn't feel the blow that killed him, but before that... well."

"When?" I asked.

"Taking into account the fact that he'd been in the water for more than a day, I'd say... late Saturday, early Sunday. Probably between nine o'clock on Saturday evening and, say, five on Sunday morning. Because of the water I can't be more precise."

"Any idea how many?"

"How many people beat him? No. More than one, I'd say, but...."

"Did you find anything on the body that would indicate where it happened?"

"No. His clothes were covered in debris, all of it waterborne. There's no telling where he was put into the river, either. It could have been anywhere from Harrison on down. The current is quite slow up there, so anywhere between the Booker T. Washington State Park and the coastguard station. My guess though, and it's a wild one, would be Webb Road just west of the park, or even inside the park itself, say Champion Road. As I said, though, it's only a guess."

I said nothing more. Not because I didn't want to, but because I couldn't focus. My guts were in turmoil; my head was still numb. I got up, grabbed Amanda's hand, pulled her to her feet, and headed for the door. Kate stayed for a moment—to speak to Sheddon, I supposed—but she followed a minute or so later, and caught up with us in the parking lot.

"Harry," she said, "we need to talk. I know you, and I know what's going on inside you. You can't do what you're planning. You go off on some kind of crazy crusade and I can't—I *won't* help you, and I won't be able to protect you. It's officially my case. Let me handle it. I'll keep you up to speed, but you have to leave it to us."

When she saw the look on my face she must have known she was pissing in the wind. It wasn't going to happen, and she knew it. He was my brother, and it would be me who....

"Sure, Kate," I said. "I understand. We're going home now. I need to get some rest. I still have a company to run, right?"

"Shit," she said. "Here we go. I'm warning you, Harry. I can't let you do this."

I smiled at her. Well, it was meant to be a smile. It was probably more of a grimace.

"Come on, Kate. You and I both know how it works.

You'll do your thing. You'll find nothing. Three months from now the case will be cold and sitting on a shelf in some back room at the PD. Right?"

She didn't answer. We'd both seen it so many times before. It was one of the reasons I'd quit the force in the first place: hands tied, bureaucracy, politics, you name it. I withstood it for almost nine years, during most of which Kate had been my partner, and then I'd had it with the system. I quit and formed my own private investigation agency. Since then, Kate, now a lieutenant in the Major Crimes Unit, had remained a sort of pseudo partner, an insider at the PD with whom I was privileged to work on occasion, the latest being the disappearance of the Chief Johnston's daughter. I'd found the pigs responsible for her death, and by God I'd find those responsible for Henry's.

I told Kate, "Call me tomorrow. On my cell phone. I'll keep *you* up to speed." Then I opened the car door for Amanda, nodded to Kate, and then I headed to Riverview Road where I picked up Rose and my father—I needed to gather what was left of my little family together. There was no way I could leave them to grieve alone; we would do that as a family, at home.

5

Tuesday Morning, Early

I hardly slept at all that night. I lay on top of the covers with Amanda snuggled in close to me. She slept, but only fitfully. By four o'clock in the morning, I was outside seated on the patio with a cup of coffee, staring down at the lights of a city that didn't seem quite so friendly anymore.

I'd only been there a few minutes when she slipped her hands over my shoulders, down my chest, and laid her cheek against the top of my head.

"Sit," I said, looking up at her. She slipped onto the bench beside and sat, feet apart, knees together, with her hands clasped in her lap.

"You want coffee?" I asked.

She shook her head.

"Somewhere down there," I said after a moment, "sleeping without a care in the world, are the bastards that killed Henry. I'm going to find them, Amanda, and when I do—"

"You can't," she told me. "You heard what Kate said. You'll go to jail for the rest of your life."

I smiled, sipped on my coffee, said nothing. I put my arm around her and pulled her in close. She was soft and warm, and she smelled heavenly, and any other time.... That night, however, what was left of it, was different. I just needed to hold her. So I did.

I didn't run that next morning. August and Rose joined us on the patio around six, and we just watched the sun rise, sitting quietly side by side. I held Amanda's hand, August held Rose's, and we sat there speaking hardly at all for more than an hour. God only knew what was going on their heads. For sure I knew what was going on in mine, and it wasn't pretty.

Amanda made breakfast around seven, not that any of us wanted to eat. She said it seemed to be the thing to do. We ate in silence. I drank three cups of coffee. Rose was... well, I dunno. How can you know?

Finally, Amanda spoke. "Harry, talk to me."

"About what?"

"Oh God, you know what. What are you going to do?"

At that, Rose and my father both looked at me. It was the question they both had been waiting for.

"I'm going to find them, the people responsible for Henry's murder, but you knew that, so why ask?" It came across harshly, not at all like I'd wanted. Amanda looked at me like I'd slapped her in the face. "I'm sorry. That's not what I meant. I'm so damned.... Shit, I don't know what I am. I'm sorry, Amanda."

She looked mollified, but I wasn't sure, so I reached out and took her hand and kissed it.

"It will be all right," I whispered. "I promise...."

Yeah, but will it?

I thought for a moment, and then decided they needed a little more than I could give, at least right then, but I tried.

"It shouldn't be too difficult—to find them, I mean. It takes a certain kind of low life to do something like this, and they'll need to talk about it, brag about it. They always do. It's a street thing; builds cred among the bangers. Word will be on the street, even now. People talk; people listen. Two days, no more, and I'll know. You'll see. Now, Amanda. I need to go to the office. I need you to stay here with my mom and dad. I'll be back as soon as I can—" and at that, Rose started crying again. I'd never called her that before. It was kind of out there, her being as young as she was, but it somehow seemed appropriate just then.

"Why?" Amanda asked. "Why do you have to go to work today? Surely—"

I gave her hand a squeeze. "No, I'm not going to work. I won't, not until this thing is done with, and.... I just need to make sure they have everything they need to carry on without me. And I need to make some calls. I'll be back before you know it."

I turned to my parents. "You guys stay here 'till this is over. No arguments. Two, maybe three days. That's all. I want you where I know you'll be okay. Amanda will look after you both. Now, I have to go."

It was almost nine o'clock when I walked into the office that morning. It was silent as a tomb. Oh, everyone was there, but no one was talking.

"It's okay, folks," I told them. "I'm okay. Life goes on and so do we. I just need to take a few days off, look after my parents. I only came in to make sure you have everything you need. Bob, Jacque, I need a few minutes with both of you, in my office, please."

I spent the next thirty minutes explaining to them what had happened to Henry and how I was going to take a few days off, and then I explained what their duties would be while I was gone.

"Jacque, for you there won't be much change in your daily routine. Bob, you'll take over my role. It shouldn't be for more than three or four days, but I need to know things here will continue on as usual. Okay?"

They both nodded; they both sat there staring at me. It was Bob who spoke first.

"Jacque," he said, "I'd like to talk to Harry alone, if you don't mind."

"Hah, you tink?"

Oh hell, there's the accent. She's pissed.

"You tink you de only one who give a damn. I'm stayin' put."

Bob looked at her and smiled. He knew her as well as I did. There would be nothing done without Jacque being a part of it. She's been my personal assistant since before she got out of college. She's thirty years old, but looks nineteen. She's Jamaican, beautiful, and... gay, something I only found out recently. She has a master's degree in business administration and a bachelor's in criminology, but that's not why I hired her. I hired her because I thought she could do the job, and because I liked her.

Bob nodded at her. She smiled at him. They both turned to look at me.

"What?" I asked.

"Talk to us, Harry," Bob said.

I shook my head. "I can't. What I'm about to do could at worst get me killed, and at best put me behind bars. You don't need to even know."

"You crazy son of a bitch," Bob growled. "After what we've been through together? If you think you can go after them on your own, without me, you're friggin' nuts. If you think you can leave me out of this—"

"This is different, Bob. I never intended to kill anyone before—"

"Yeah, but you did. *We* did. I pulled your ass out of the fire more than a couple of times, same as you did mine. Harry, you don't have a say in this one. You try leaving me out, I'll quit my job right here and now and go after them alone. Your folks already lost Henry; you think.... It ain't gonna happen, brother."

Brother? I smiled. *That's another first.*

When I looked at Jacque, she was nodding slowly. "You heard the man. What he said, I say."

"*Both* of you? Jacque, I can't have you out there—"

"You want my notice in writin', or will word of mout' do?"

"Jacque, we're talking violence here, probably deadly violence."

"I know that. And you know I can handle it."

And she was right. She could handle a firearm better than most, and she had a black belt in Krav Maga, courtesy of Heather Stillwell, my other senior investigator. Still....

"Okay." I said it reluctantly, but I knew they both meant what they said. "But nothing said in this office leaves here, right?"

Oh my God, Jacque too. What the hell am I thinking?

They both nodded.

It was right about then that my cell phone rang. I didn't recognize the number, and I almost ignored the call, but fortunately I didn't.

"Harry, is that you?"

Benny Hinkle? What the hell?

Benny was the last person I would have expected to hear from. You'd have to know him to understand. He's not all he appears to be, a weird little creep... ah, not so little, more a fat bastard than little. Anyway, he's the greasy slob who owns and runs the Sorbonne, a so-called downtown nightclub that the cops say is the original butthole of the seedy side of the city. Be that as it may, Benny is as sharp as a tack and the two of us have enjoyed... well, maybe not enjoyed, a symbiotic though somewhat tenuous relationship for more years than I can remember.

"Benny, this is not a good time."

"Yeah, I know. I heard about your brother. I'm sorry. Look, we gotta talk, an' quick."

"Talk about what?" I looked over the desk at Bob and Jacque. They were watching me questioningly. I shrugged.

"Not over the phone, Harry, an' not here. I'll come see you. I'll be at your offices in ten minutes; leave that damn gate open for me. I don't want anybody to see me, okay?" And then he hung up, leaving me more than a little baffled.

"Was that Benny Hinkle?" Bob asked. "What the hell was that about?"

"The hell if I know, but we will soon. He's on his way here."

Bob was astounded. "Here? He never crawls out of that cesspit he calls a bar. What the hell can he want?"

The answer was soon forthcoming. I met Benny at the side door, inside the small compound that is my office parking lot, the product of another now almost forgotten conflict with the denizens of our fair city.

He came skittering in through the open door like a fat rat on the run from a hungry cat. He reached the doorway, stopped, turned, looked furtively around, then backed all the way in and slammed the door behind him. He was breathing hard, like just he'd run a marathon.

"Whew." He grinned up at me. He was all of five foot eight. "That was exciting. Where can we talk?"

I looked him up and down, sighed, and said, "In my office. It's this way."

"Hey, Bob," Benny smirked as he slipped by me, sideways, into my office. "How's the private dick business?" Bob gave him a look that would have petrified most mortals, but one of those Benny is not.

He dropped his fat ass into one of my expensively upholstered guest chairs—I shuddered to think what grease and filth he might be depositing—and he gazed fondly at Jacque.

"Well now, Harry. Who's this lovely young slip of a girl?"

I looked at her and shook my head.

She got the message. "I'm Jacque Hale, Mr. Starke's personal assistant."

"Whoooh, Mr. Starke. Personal assistant. How fine and high and mighty."

"That's enough, Benny. What do you want?"

"Well, as I said on the phone, I heard about your brother. I'm sorry, Harry. He was good little kid. Used to come into the club now and then. Never caused any trouble. Went off the track a bit, but don't we all? Okay, okay. I'm gettin' to it. There's talk, talk on the street. Hell, they was yackin', in my bar, last night for Christ's sake. Duvon James has been braggin' about how he done it. Never could keep his mouth shut, that one...."

"What?" I leaned toward him. "What the hell are you talking about? They left town more than two years ago when Harper went down. All three of them did: Shady, Duvon, and the creepy little bastard, uh... Gold."

"Yeah, well, they's back. Have been for more'n a year. Shady's still working for Harper. Well, his daughter an' her lawyer husband."

I stared at him over the desk. I could hardly believe what he was telling me. "How do I not know about this?" I asked.

He shrugged. "Dunno. Well yeah, I do. They bin keepin' a really low profile. The Greenes"—he shrugged—"I thought everyone knew they was runnin' Harper's empire now that he's a guest of the government."

"Well yeah, but I didn't know that Tree was back. I guess it makes sense, though. He never was charged with anything. Benny, you piece of garbage. Why didn't you tell me he was back?"

He shrugged, looked sheepishly down at his feet, then said, "Dunno. Didn't think it mattered."

"So what's he doing for them, the Greenes?"

"Not sure. Drugs, I think."

"So Duvon James in the Sorbonne, huh?" I asked thoughtfully.

"Look, Harry. I don't know. Street talk is he's braggin' about how he done Harry Starke's baby brother—"

My blood ran cold.

"An' put him... in the river," Benny continued, warily. "Harry, the word is John Greene's put a contract out on you, which is why I didn't want you in my place, an' why I didn't wanna be seen talkin' to you."

A contract. Scary? You bet, but it wasn't the first time. And, as they say, forewarned is forearmed.

"Thanks Benny. How much?"

"Oh you don't owe me.... Oh, you mean the contract? Twen'y-five large."

I nodded.

"What do you know about them, Benny?"

"The Greenes? Not a whole lot. They also like to keep outa sight an' outa mind."

"No, Benny. Not the Greenes. Them I know about. Shady and his goons. What are they up to? Where are they holed up? Are they on their own? What?"

He shook his head. "There you have me, Harry. I know they're here somewhere, but where... I don't know. You'd better be watchin' your ass is all I can say."

"Okay, Benny. Here's what I want you to do—"

"Now hold on there, big fella. I ain't getting' involved in any of this. You're on your own."

"You're already involved, Benny. You involved yourself the minute you picked up the phone and called me. You think they don't, or won't, know you ratted on them?"

"I didn't rat on any... oh yeah, I suppose I did." He heaved a big sigh. "Okay, whadda you want?"

"I want to know where Shady is operating from—where he's holed up—how many people he has working for him, and what he's doing for the Greenes. You give me that and I'll end this thing fast. I want it today, tonight at the latest. You have my cell number. Call anytime. I'll be waiting. Now get out of here."

He jumped to his feet and headed for the door.

"Hey, Benny, wait."

He stopped in the doorway, turned. "What?"

"Thanks."

He nodded. "You owe me, Starke.... Nah, you don't; you're welcome." Then he turned again and was gone, leaving the three of us staring at the open door. Finally, Jacque got up and closed it.

"Still want in?" I asked them both as she returned to her seat.

They nodded.

"Well, you heard him. Thoughts?"

"Well," Bob said, "the good news, if there is any, is that we know they're after you. We'll be ready. I think maybe I should come and stay up at your house until this thing is done, maybe Jacque too. Together we stand, divided we fall, right?"

I thought about it, and in part I agreed with the idea. There were a couple of problems, though. One of them was Amanda, the other my father.

"I can't have my folks and Amanda knowing about any of this," I said. "I don't know how we could hide it from them if you two are up at the house."

"Not a good idea, boss," Jacque said. "Don't you dare lie to Amanda. Tell her the truth. They all know what you are and what you do. They're used to it. They'll understand."

I thought some more, nodded, and said, "Okay. It's a plan. But before we leave we'll put Heather in the picture. She'll have to hold down the fort while we see this thing through. Now, let's get prepped."

We left my office and headed down the corridor, past Tim's cyber world to the small strong room where we kept the weapons and... other things. I entered the code on the touchpad and spun the lock.

I grabbed three large, black canvas holdalls from one

of the shelves and dumped them on the steel table in the center of the room.

"Vests first," I said, reaching for a Point Blank Spider Tactical vest I thought might fit Jacque and handing it to her. "Try that on. It needs to be snug, but not too tight."

She stripped off her jacket and slipped it on: perfect. Mine and Bob's were on hangers. All three vests went in the bags, one in each.

"Jacque, I think maybe a Glock 19. It holds fifteen rounds. And a Glock 26. It only holds ten, but it's small and light."

I handed the two weapons to her along with an Appendix carry holster and a Blackhawk ankle holster. She slipped them into her bag.

Bob picked out a full-size Sig .45 1911 to go with the compact model he usually carried. Both had been fitted with Storm Lake threaded barrels to accommodate suppressors, as had most of the weapons in the closet, including the ones I'd just handed Jacque.

Me? I dumped my M&P9 in favor of a matched pair of Sig full-size .45 1911s with standard seven-round mags. I also grabbed three twelve-round extended mags. Those I would carry with me.

I looked at Bob. "Long guns?"

He nodded and reached for a Remington 870 shotgun with a pistol grip. I put a hand on his arm to stop him. "Too noisy. We don't want to attract attention."

He nodded and reached instead for a Tavor IDF16 semi-automatic rifle fitted with holographic sights, the Israeli "Bullpup."

I nodded approvingly. I loved that rifle. It was short, only twenty-six inches long—the chamber was way back inside the stock. The standard mag held thirty rounds of .223. It was short, light, and deadly, and it was my choice too. Three sets of night-vision goggles, five Surefire LED flashlight/laser units for the handguns, and we were done. We packed everything away in the bags along with extra mags and suppressors for all of the weapons, and then I had a thought. I grabbed a half dozen units of Freeze+P spray and threw them into my bag. You never know. We grabbed the bags, closed up the strong room door, and then headed out into the parking lot, stopping only to loop Heather Stillwell in and put her in charge of the company.

But it wasn't quite that simple. Jacque's partner, Wendy, had to be appraised of what we were about to do. I offered to do it, but Jacque insisted on doing it herself.

"Besides," she said, "I have to get clothes and toiletries."

I nodded. "Clothes you need, toiletries you don't. Amanda has enough stuff up there open a store."

Bob had no such responsibilities. He got the easy task of heading up the mountain in his ancient Jeep Grand Wagoneer, which was good, but I needed to get there first. I had some serious explaining to do before my little army arrived. So I asked him to stop off on the way for thirty minutes or so and grab a coffee while I did the deed. And he did.

As I drove on up Scenic Highway toward home, I tossed what I was about to say around in my head, trying to come up with a way to tell them that wouldn't cause them too much concern. It was a stupid exercise. Nothing I could think of made it sound good. In the end I decided to just come right on out with it. I parked the Maxima in the garage and went through the house to the patio at the back, where I found them sitting together. The ladies were sipping fruit cocktails; the old man had his usual gin and tonic.

"I need to talk to you all," I said, dumping myself down in a wicker chair beside Amanda. Oh yeah, I needed to get this off my chest, and quickly.

I explained everything I'd learned just as it had been told to me, even the contract Greene had put on my head, and I watched as the looks on their faces grew more and more horrified, and then I told them about the plan. How Bob and Jacque had insisted on joining me, and that they were on their way up the mountain even as we spoke, and I was relieved to see the looks of horror turn into looks of concern. They didn't know Jacque that well, but they did know Bob.

Amanda, now somewhat mollified, took my hand and led me into the house. Nope, it wasn't what you're thinking. All she wanted to do was hold me, and I wanted nothing more either. For maybe five minutes we stood together, talking, and then we heard Bob's old Jeep rattle onto the property.

He jumped out, grabbed the holdall from the back, and carried it over his shoulder into the house. Bob's an ex-marine and a one-time cop, but sometimes I can almost forget it because he's so quiet. But watching him come into the house then, I remembered.

Amanda showed him to one of the guest rooms, and less than five minutes later she was showing Jacque to hers.

And that was it. All we had to do after that was wait for Benny to call. And wait we did.

We had lunch outside on the patio—salads all around, much to Bob's disgust.

"Grazing, that's what it is," he growled. "You got any decent bread? I'll make myself a cheese and onion sandwich."

So that was what he had, and after we ate we sipped sodas by the pool and waited some more. The conversation was sparse. We were after all an eclectic bunch, and we were all trying to watch what we said in front of Rose and my father.

Finally, Bob got to his feet, stepped to the edge of the pool, and said, "Well now. I'm not gonna waste an opportunity like this. You got spare trunks or do I go in in my shorts?"

"In the pool house," Amanda said. And then, smiling, "Although the shorts might be—"

"Okay, okay," I said. "That's enough. You'll find spares in the pool house. Jacque, there are several that will fit you too."

They went off together, to find something suitable, I assumed. Rose watched them go and then got to her feet and went into the house; Amanda followed her. When they returned a few minutes later, I was a little surprised to see that Rose was wearing one of Amanda's bikinis.

She walked down the steps into the pool and then swam with long, slow strokes to the far end, where she stopped, put her elbows on the tiles, and laid her head on her arms.

I looked at Amanda quizzically, but she just shrugged and went back into the house. Bob and Jacque joined Rose in the water, and I left August staring vacantly out toward the horizon where the cooling towers of the Sequoya Nuclear Plant were just visible, shimmering in the distant haze.

I met Amanda in the kitchen. She was in a pensive mood, quiet, thoughtful.

"Hey," I said, tilting her chin up a little with my finger. "You all right?"

"No, you ass. Of course I'm not. I don't want you to do this, Harry. They'll kill you."

"Me?" I asked lightly. "Not hardly." I leaned forward and brushed her lips with mine. She turned her head away.

"I can't stand it," she said, in a low voice.

"I know, honey, but I don't have a choice. Greene wants me dead. My only chance is to beat them to it. A good offense is the best defense, right? As soon as Benny tells me what I need to know, we'll go after them. Take them by surprise. Hell, Amanda, I have Bob, the best defense any man could ask for. You can attest to that. And I have Jacque, too. So don't worry. It will all be over in a couple of days."

She stood there, staring into my eyes, her own watering. Then without a word, she took my hand and led me into our bedroom... and she made love to me that afternoon as if there would be no tomorrow. Maybe there wouldn't be.

6

Tuesday, Mid-Afternoon

That Tuesday afternoon dragged on like no other. We sat around, waiting. No one wanted to talk. Jacque and Amanda sat by the pool. Bob prowled the gardens like a restless tiger. August and Rose disappeared into the house. Me? I was as restless as Bob. A half dozen times I was tempted to call Benny, but I knew it would be pointless; he would call when he had something.

I looked at my watch. It was a little after two thirty. *Jeez, I can't stand much more of this. I have to do something!*

I went into the house and changed clothes—tan pants, black golf shirt, and a lightweight tan golf jacket to hide the twin shoulder rigs housing the two 1911s. I slipped my Talon expandable baton into my pants pocket and then walked through the house, into the garage, and unlocked the Maxima.

"Where do you think you're going?" Bob was standing in the open garage door, his bulk almost filling it.

"I thought I'd go get something for dinner," I told him. "Save the girls having to cook."

"Dinner? Wearing that double rig?"

I glanced down. The jacket was open just enough to reveal the grips. "It's not what you're thinking. There's a contract out on me, right? Be kinda stupid to leave 'em here, don't you think?"

"You're so damned full of it, it's a wonder you don't bust wide open." He walked into the garage and climbed into the passenger seat of the Maxima. I shook my head.

"Well," he said through the open driver's-side door, "we going or not?"

I said nothing. I climbed in and hit the starter button, reversed out, shoved the selector into drive, and spun out of the driveway, almost hitting the still-opening electronic gates in the process.

I'd barely reached Scenic Highway when the interior of the car virtually exploded with noise. An incoming call. Damned Bluetooth—I never could remember to turn the friggin' sound down.

I hit the button to take the call, and Amanda's voice boomed out from the speakers.

"Where the hell are you going, and why didn't you tell me?"

"I thought I'd go get some dinner for everybody. I

know you don't want to cook." I looked at Bob. He grinned back at me. I shrugged.

"Your damn guns are missing!" she yelled. "Jacque checked!"

"That's true, sweetie. You know I never go anywhere without them," I said.

Bob rolled his eyes.

"Listen," I said. "I can't talk. I'm heading down the mountain, and you know what the road is like. I won't be long, I promise."

"If you're just going to get dinner, why is Bob with you?"

"I was bored," Bob said. "I needed out for a little while."

Amanda was silent for a moment, and then said, "Okay, but be careful. Drive safely." And then she hung up.

"You know you're gonna pay for that lie, don't you?" Bob asked.

"Yeah well. What she doesn't know ain't gonna hurt her. And I *will* bring dinner home. But before that, there's someone I want to see."

I stepped on the gas, screeched around the hairpin, and roared off the feeder onto Cummings Highway. Ten minutes later I was downtown shoving quarters into the meter outside the Tower Building.

7

Tuesday Afternoon 3pm

We rode the elevator to the top floor of the building, but we didn't go in immediately. For a moment I stood in front of the door, Bob behind me, remembering. Back in the day, this suite had been the world headquarters of Congressman Gordon "Little Billy" Harper's spurious empire. I thought of the people he'd ruined, and those who'd died because of him: the beautiful Charlie Maxwell, Olivia Hansen, and Michael Falk, whom I had never met, but most of all I remembered Tabitha and that moment I'd met her on the Walnut Street Bridge, and my blood boiled. *Was Little Billy Harper in some way responsible for what had happened to Henry? If he was... if he....*

It was no more than a few seconds until I looked around at Bob. He knew what was going on in my head, and when he nodded I barged straight in, past the startled receptionist, through the double doors, into the Greenes' inner sanctum. As I pushed open the doors I had another of those moments where actions long forgotten come flooding back. I'd come through those doors just the same way about two years ago. In my mind's eye I could see Harper sitting there behind the huge glass desk, a self-satisfied smirk on his face. To his right, Jackson Hope, his bodyguard-cum-financial-advisor, had been seated at an incongruously small writing desk.

The two desks were still there. Harper and Hope were not. Instead, Harper's daughter, Kathryn Greene, had taken his place behind the glass desk, and her husband, Jonathan Greene—lawyer, lobbyist, now seemingly head of some sort of homegrown crime family, and all-around worthless piece of garbage—was seated where Hope had once fiddled the books for her father. This time, though, the desk was a little bigger, even if the man wasn't. And he was quick. Too quick for me to stop him when his right hand flashed out and hit the button on the side of his desk.

"Bad move, Johnny Boy," I said as I stepped to the right, out of line of sight of the door behind me. Bob moved quickly to the left and took up a position with his back to the window facing the big glass desk. My move had put me against the wall maybe eight feet from Greene's desk.

Quick as we were, we had barely made it before the doors burst open and two gorillas barreled in. When I say gorillas, maybe I was exaggerating just a little. One was tall, skinny, and white. The other was not so tall, nor was he skinny; he was also Hispanic.

"Whoa," Bob said lightly, waving one of his 1911s in their faces, the hammer already cocked. "Slow down, boys. You're not going to miss anything, I promise." And they did slow down. In fact, they froze. I almost smiled. The two of them reminded me of Wile E. Coyote and the Road Runner—you know the scene. They're both running flat out and then suddenly they're frozen in midair, legs outstretched. These two gorillas were leaned forward, arms extended, and if the situation had been different it would have been downright funny. As it was... well, it was not.

"Easy Jason, Miguel," Kathryn said, holding up her hand.

"Yeah," I said as I slid behind them. "Very easy." I relieved them of a total of five handguns: two Glocks, two revolvers, and a tiny Derringer I found sticking out of the top of one of Miguel's boots. Then I stepped back to the window, opened it, and looked down. Ten floors below I could see an open dumpster. I tossed the five pieces out and watched as they clattered into the empty bin. I closed the window, turned, and walked toward Kathryn. Johnny swiveled his chair and rolled across to join his wife. His face was white; he was angry, but hers... well, she didn't seem to be the slightest bit perturbed. Or maybe she was, and just better at hiding it than her husband.

"You boys need to step over there," I said to Wile E. and the Bird with a smile. "Go stand in the corner 'till I say you can come out." Slowly, with hands held high, they did as they were told, Bob watching every move. His 1911 never wavered.

"Now, Kathryn," I said, dragging up a chair and sitting down. "It seems we have a little problem. Eh, several problems, in fact, and none of them *really* little."

She glared at me, as did her husband, but said nothing.

"No comment?" I asked. "Well then, let's discuss things, shall we?"

Again, they didn't answer.

"I understand that you've taken over Little Billy's empire."

No answer.

"Now look," I said. "It's very rude not to answer when you're asked a direct question. I don't like rude people, and I know Bob doesn't. Right, Bob?"

He nodded once, never taking his eyes off Wile E. and the Runner.

"So, I'll ask you once more, and if you don't answer, I'll hurt your husband Johnny here." I waved my hand in the general direction of the now chalk-faced Jonathan Greene. "So what's it to be?"

"You wouldn't dare," she snarled.

I reached into my pocked, flipped open the Talon baton, and slammed it down on the back of John Boy's hand. It wasn't that hard of a blow, but he howled like his namesake—Coyote—standing in the corner. He jumped up from the seat and backed up to the wall, nursing his hand. I collapsed the baton, though I didn't return it to my pocket.

"Yes! Okay, yes." She spit it out through clenched teeth. "I'm running my father's business until he gets out on appeal."

"That's much better," I said. Then, lightly, "So it has come to my attention that one Lester Tree, known to one and all as Shady, is back in town and working for you. Isn't that right?"

No answer. I began to rise slowly to my feet—

"Yes!" Greene said, his voice an octave higher. "That is, no—I mean yes. He's back, but he's not working for us."

I sat down again. "But if he's not working for you, as I have been assured he is, who the hell *is* he working for?"

"He works for us," Kathryn said, so quietly I could barely hear her.

"And in what capacity would that be?"

"No capacity," she said. "He just fills in when we need him. Nothing official. He's... casual labor, I suppose."

"Hmmm. I wonder if he knows that," I said, more to myself than to her. I leaned forward and rested my elbows on my knees and clasped my hands together in front of me, the baton between my palms. "The problem is, you see, that either Shady, or one of his low lifes, killed my kid brother. But you knew that, yes? Yes, I can see by the looks on your faces that you did.

"Now then, if Shady works for you, and if Shady is responsible for my little brother's demise, that makes you.... Well, you get the idea. You're a lawyer, right? A particularly nasty member of the species, but a lawyer nonetheless. Comments?"

I thought for a minute that I wasn't going to get an answer, but then Greene said, "I have no idea what the hell you're talking about."

Kathryn was shaking her head.

"That's what I thought you'd say. You don't, I suppose, have any idea where the erstwhile Mr. Tree might be found, do you? No, of course you don't. Well, never mind. We'll find him, sooner if not later."

I looked at him, and then at her. He was shaking. She was the proverbial ice maiden. The look on her face could have frozen pump water.

"You're being rude again," I said in a singsong voice.

"I'm sure you will find him," she said. "Anything else, Mr. Starke? If not, I'd like you to leave."

"Yeah well. What you want and what you get, huh? No, I'm not finished yet. There's the other little problem we need to discuss." Again I looked at them both, waiting.

She frowned. "And what might that be?"

I sucked air in noisily through my teeth, then said, "I think Mr. Greene is the person to answer that question."

She looked sideways at him, and I saw it immediately. *She doesn't know. Hah!*

He knew, though. The twitch at the left corner of his mouth told me he did.

"Tell her," I said coldly.

"Tell her what?"

I sighed, got to my feet, walked to the window, looked out, then back at him. "Tell her."

"Tell her *what*, dammit. I don't know what the hell you're talking about."

I nodded, then began to walk slowly toward him. I flipped the baton open. As I drew closer, he cowered back until he was almost leaning on his wife, his hands up to shield his face. I stopped in front of him, looked at the red mark on his hand where the baton had connected earlier.

"Last chance, Johnny."

"I don't—aaaargh!"

I brought the baton around in a fast backhand swing, as hard as I could against his right wrist. The crack as the bone broke was sickening, even to me. His wife jumped to her feet, looking wildly around for something, I had no idea what.

"Sit *down*," I shouted at her. "Your piece of shit husband has put out a contract on me. Twenty-five thousand goddamn dollars."

She didn't sit, but she looked like she'd been stabbed. The look, first one of shock and then of anger, was something to see. Kathryn Greene screwed up her face and yelled, "You *stupid son of a bitch*." And then she punched him, hard. The blow connected with his left ear and all but knocked his head from his shoulders. He staggered sideways and rolled along the wall holding his wrist, howling like a dog. I closed the baton and slipped it back into my pocket

Kathryn's anger was, however, like a donkey's gallop, soon over, and she dropped back down into her chair, flapping her hand to relieve the pain in her knuckles. She put her elbows on the desktop and let her head drop into her hands, and sat quietly, but only for a few seconds. Soon enough she had come up out of her hands, all business. She straightened the collar of her jacket and looked up at me.

"I don't know if what you say is true. If it is, I didn't know about it. If it is true, the contract will be lifted immediately." She twisted round in her seat, scowled down at her husband, and said, "See to it."

He nodded, still nursing his wrist. His ear was the color of a rotten tomato. It would probably look like a cauliflower by morning.

"Now then, Mr. Starke," she said, briskly. "If there's nothing more, I suggest you leave. I'll have Jason and Miguel clean up the mess." Again she looked at her husband. "Please close the door behind you."

And we did.

"Jeez, Harry," Bob said as we rode down in the elevator. "I didn't know you had that thing with you. Nice stroke, by the way. What did you say your handicap was?"

"Hmmm, on a good day, nine. Never more than ten."

He grinned, then shook his head. "Damned if I don't believe you. And did you see his ear? Damn it, Harry, I'd like to get to know that lady. I wonder if I should ask her out." *He's joking, of course, I think.*

I grinned at him. "Bob, I actually believe you'd do that."

"You betcha. Maybe when this is done with, I will. So what now?" he asked as we climbed into the car.

"Dinner. What else? Hell, I can't go back up there without it, now can I?"

"Guess not."

"Chinese sound good? I want a little General Tso's Chicken, and maybe some dim sum, some hot and sour soup, and crispy noodles. We'll get some sweet 'n' sour chicken, chicken in garlic sauce, fried rice, steamed rice—and how about some egg rolls? I like egg rolls. Jeez, Bob, I'm starving."

He looked sideways at me, shaking his head as I headed for P.F. Chang's.

"You're feeling better, right?"

I grinned back at him, but I didn't answer. I didn't need to.

8

Tuesday Evening, Late

The rest of the afternoon passed slowly. By nine o'clock Benny still hadn't called, and we were all on edge. Eventually I gave in and called him. I knew there'd be few people, if any, in the Sorbonne that early on a weekday.

The phone rang on and on interminably. I was just about to hang it up when his partner, Laura, answered.

"Sorbonne."

"Hey, Laura. It's Harry Starke. Where's your little friend?"

"Hello, Harry. You mean Benny? He's not here. He ain't been here all day. Do you have any idea how much work it is getting this place ready to open each day? Of course you don't. You're a man. So whadda ya want me to tell him when he gets here, if he ever does?"

Crap. Where the hell is he?

"Nothing. Just tell him I called. Have a good evening, Laura."

"You too, hun."

I wasn't surprised, and I really shouldn't have called, but what the hell; I was in one of those moods. I was restless and impatient, and I needed to get over it and settle down. Right about then a stiff measure of Laphroaig would probably have set me right, but I didn't dare; I didn't know what the rest of the night might hold. I just had to get a grip and... what else I had no idea.

We were all still outside at ten o'clock that evening, seated around the pool, enjoying one of the finest views in five states. The city lights were at their brightest. The great river twinkled and shimmered as it curved first to the left and then to the right around the far eastern edge of the twinkling panorama. Life would have been good if not for the dark cloud hanging over us, a cloud that wouldn't lift until I'd finished with Tree and his gang of villains.

At ten thirty, I went into the house, changed into swim trunks, and headed back out to the pool. I dived into the water from the springboard and settled into a slow, rhythmic crawl that propelled me rapidly from one end of the pool to the other. By the time I'd finished swimming laps I was feeling somewhat better, but Benny still hadn't called, and I was getting worried.

I hope to hell nothing's happened to the fat little bastard.

Slowly, one after another, the others headed into the house, leaving me alone with Amanda. I went and turned off the floodlights. Except for the underwater lights in the pool, and those of the city far below, it was quite dark.

And once again my thoughts turned to Henry. The pool reminded me of the good times we'd all had at the family gatherings at my father's house on Riverview Road. Henry, goofy little Hank, had been a big part of them.

I turned my head to speak to Amanda, to reminisce, but she leaned toward me and placed a finger on my lips and shook her head. She understood. She rose, went to the steps, tested the temperature with her toe, then stepped down into the water and swam a slow breast stroke from one end of the pool to the other and back again, the underwater lights throwing her body into stark relief; she was a black shadow moving across the rippling surface of the water. She swam to the edge of the pool in front of me and beckoned. I smiled and shook my head. She shrugged, turned in the water, pushed off and swam to the far side of the pool and in a single fluid motion, hoisted herself out of the water, onto the top of the infinity wall. She stood there for a moment with her back to me, feet apart, staring down at the city lights, which provided just enough of a glow to outline her body. She was wearing her favorite pink bikini; it left little to the imagination. And the droplets of water on her shoulders and in her hair shone like colored jewels.

She sat down along the top of the wall, threw back her head, and shook out her hair. She was a lovely silhouette against the glittering city, and from this that angle she seemed to be sitting on top of the water—an optical illusion, but a breathtakingly beautiful one.

How long I sat there watching her, I have no idea. I was away with the birds, if you will; my mind drifting back and forth over the past three years that I'd known her, the extraordinary circumstances that had brought us together. My brother's death had brought my feelings for Amanda sharply into focus, and I knew, then more than ever before, that I loved her dearly, and wanted to spend the rest of my life with her.

I lay on my lounger watching her and listened to the night. For a moment or two I was even at peace. Only the dull murmur of the insects and the gentle lapping of the water disturbed the stillness of the night. I think Amanda must have been able to feel me staring at her, because she turned her head, lowered it, looked at me through her eyelashes, and smiled that special smile.

I smiled back her, lay my head back, closed my eyes and... suddenly I felt the hair on the back of my neck begin to prickle, and I was overwhelmed by a horrible feeling that something was wrong. I had no idea what brought it on. I'd heard nothing... and maybe that was it; maybe it was *too* quiet.

I opened my eyes, instantly alert, and stood and looked out over the pool down the slope into the gardens. Nothing. It was dark down there, but....

What the hell is that?

Somewhere down the slope, beyond the stone wall that formed the perimeter of the gardens, something was moving. And then I heard it: the sharp crack of a twig snapping underfoot.

I gestured for Amanda to get off the wall. I needn't have bothered. She'd heard the sound too, and had already slipped noiselessly into the water.

I met her on my hands and knees at the poolside, gave her my hand, and in a single swift, fluid movement I hauled her out of the water. She came up like an arrow; she almost flew up beside me.

Crack. There it was again.

"Quick," I whispered. "Into the house."

I held her hand as we ran, heads down, through the open door.

"Get Rose and Dad and take them to the panic room."

She nodded, then turned and ran through the house, water flying in all directions.

Oh yeah, we had one of those, a panic room. She'd thought I was paranoid when I suggested we have one built into the basement. I'm sure she was glad of it then, though.

I ran down the hall and barged into Bob's room. He was snoring like a hog. My intention was to shake him awake, but before I could, he was up and had me by the throat, the barrel of a 1911 pushing into the side of my neck. I didn't know whether to be pissed or impressed; I settled for the latter.

"Christ, Bob. It's me. Lemme go for God's sake."

And he did. "You should know better than to creep

up on me in the middle of the night, buddy," he growled, and the pressure on my neck relaxed.

"So you weren't asleep?"

"I never sleep. What's up?"

"I'm not sure. There's someone creeping around out there, on the slopes beyond the garden wall."

He nodded, climbed out of bed, slipped into a T-shirt and a pair of loafers, and grabbed both of his 1911s. "Let's take a look."

"Wait. I need to—"

"Nah, you don't. Take one of these." He tossed one of the Sigs to me. "Let's go see who's out there."

We stood in the shadows under the canopy at the rear of the pool house, and listened. There was someone out there all right. We hadn't been there but a couple of seconds when I spotted a shadow climb cautiously up over the top of the far perimeter wall, and then tumble down into the darkness.

Crap, I'm glad he's down there and I'm up here, I thought, hefting the heavy weapon. I nudged Bob.

"I see him," he whispered.

But there was more than just one. Over the next thirty seconds or so I counted no less than six more shadowy figures moving quickly over the wall and then up the slopes through the gardens toward the house. I looked down at the Sig in my hand and shook my head.

Seven of them, Christ. And at least one's carrying an AR. Phone! Where the hell is my phone?

It wasn't in my pants pocket. I looked around and

spotted it lying on the table by the pool, right where I'd left it when I went to fish Amanda out of the water.

"I guess Greene didn't lift the contract on me after all," I whispered. "I think we'll need to pay him and his good lady another little visit when this is over."

"Oh, we will," Bob whispered back.

"Stay here. I'll be back."

"Okay, Arnold." He grinned at me in the darkness.

I took a deep breath, then ran, head down, staying low, to the table, snatched up the phone, turned quickly, and completed the round trip. Back under the canopy, I hit the speed dial for 911.

"911 operator. What is your emergency?"

"Home invasion. At least six intruders coming through the grounds. All armed, possibly with automatic weapons."

"Where are you, sir, and what is your name?"

I gave her my name, reeled off the address, and then hung up, and just as I did, two black figures leaped up out of the shadows, over the stone balustrade onto the patio. I hit the switch and turned on floodlights, and suddenly a half acre of patio and gardens was bathed in white light. It took them completely by surprise.

One guy was teetering on edge of the infinity wall, trying to shield his eyes with one hand and find a target for what looked like an AR15 in his other. Dressed all in black from head to toe, he looked like a damned ninja; he also looked like he was walking on water.

Bob took a two-handed grip on the Sig, spread his

feet, and took aim. I put a hand on his arm, then yelled, "Give it up; the cops are on their way."

The guy on the pool wall reacted, probably in panic and, one-handed, let fly a stream of automatic fire, most of it hitting the water. *Shit, that's no AR. It's an M16 for God's sake.*

Bam! The guy on the pool wall topped over backwards into oblivion.

I felt as if I'd been hit in the head with a hammer. Bob had fired that damned .45 less than twelve inches from my left ear. But there was no time to react beyond clapping my free hand over my ear.

Bam! Bam! Bam! Bob fired three more times, the muzzle flashes fleetingly overwhelming the floods, lighting up the patio; my brain felt like a lump of concrete, and I could hear nothing.

"Son of a—" I couldn't even finish the curse. I'd spotted two more of them coming over the wall beyond the far end of the pool.

Bam, bam, bam! I fired as quickly as I could pull the trigger. The recoil of the heavy weapon slammed the grip into the heel of my hand. I hit one man high in the chest, and clipped the other's right arm as he flung himself sideways, a stream of .223s stitching their way up the pool house wall, showering us with chips of concrete.

Bob emptied his Sig into the night. I could already feel blood running down the left side of my face, courtesy of the shards of concrete.

"Go left," I yelled. "I'll go through the house and circle around the pool."

He nodded, dumped his empty mag, slammed in another, and disappeared around the corner of the building.

Involuntarily, I glanced down at my Sig. *Shit!* I ejected the mag, glanced at it, then slammed it back in. *Four left. Jeez, why didn't I grab extras? Oh well, here goes nothing.*

I sucked in a deep breath and began to back away from the pool house, trying to keep it between me and the rapidly approaching intruders.

I was almost to the sliding door when I was treated to a hail of automatic fire. The glass blew inward, shattering into thousands of tiny shards of safety glass that flew in every direction. I dived through the hole in the door, rolled across the kitchen floor, then leaped to my feet and ran through the house.

Bob? He must have been doing okay; I could see the muzzle flash of the .45 through the kitchen window.

I ran out through the front door and around the corner of the building, then had to leap back as a hail of fire from the south side of gardens tore into the stone wall above my head.

I flung myself down on my hands and knees, and when I poked my head out I spotted a dark figure running toward me.

Without thinking, I jumped to my feet, stepped out into the open, and opened fire with the Sig at exactly the same time as he did. I felt the wind of the heavy slugs as they passed over my left shoulder. I probably would have heard them too, had my ears not still been ringing. He'd missed.

I hadn't.

I saw three of my rounds hit him dead center mass. His chest literally exploded in a mist of blood and bone. He was actually lifted off his feet by the impacts and hurled over backwards. He tumbled a few yards down the slope on the right side of the pool, and then lay still.

Jesus. How many more of them? I'd now seen at least ten. *Shit. Here comes another.*

He came at me out of the darkness beyond the ornamental stone wall, moving fast and low, a wildly morphing shadow that leaped over the wall and onto the patio. He was less than fifteen feet away when I raised the Sig, and I knew right then that I was in trouble. The slide was back. The damn thing was empty.

He must have known it too, because he slowed to a walk, and then stopped maybe eight feet in front of me. I was in the dead zone—just a little too far away to make a grab for his gun, and too close for him to miss, and even beneath the black balaclava I could see he was grinning. He raised his weapon and took careful aim....

Bam! Bam! Bam! Bam! Bam! Bam!

The man shuddered and shook as the bullets tore into him, the force of the impacts jerking him like a puppet on strings. He staggered back several steps and then keeled over sideways, dead before he hit the ground, a sad heap of wasted skin, blood, and bone.

My head was pounding from the muzzle blasts and the concussion, my ears throbbing, and no wonder. When

I spun around, Jacque was standing no more than four feet behind me, feet wide apart, the Glock 19 clasped in both hands and still pointed at where the intruder had just been standing.

And then it was over. The few shadows still left on their feet melted away into the darkness, down the slopes from whence they'd come, and once again there was only the silence. After the cacophony of the last few minutes, it was almost palpable, but then I could hear the sound of approaching sirens, barely, as if at the bottom of a well. My hearing was coming back.

The attack couldn't have lasted more than five minutes, but it had seemed like an hour.

I looked at Jacque; she was white as a sheet and still frozen to the spot. I went to her.

"Hey," I said, gently pushing her hands down and taking the Glock from her. "Are you all right?"

She nodded. "Yes." She said it, but I'm still not sure she was. I put my arm around her shoulder and steered her back across the patio and into the house, through the glass-less rear doors.

Amanda met us in the kitchen. She flung her arms around my neck and squeezed like there was no tomorrow. Little did she know that there almost hadn't been.

"Stay here," I said, and disentangled myself. "I need to find Bob."

I went back outside to look for him. I didn't have to look far; he just rounding the north side of the house.

"All clear," he said. "And the cops are here."

I bent and lay Jacque's gun on the floor, and raised

my empty hands a little. Not in the "I'm guilty" position, just one in which they wouldn't shoot me on sight.

"Okay," I said. "Bob, Jacque, lay your weapons on the floor and stand still. Keep your hands where they can see them."

They came in at the rush, weapons at the ready. The search they did of the house and grounds was quick, cursory, and once it was done, and the area declared all clear, they rounded everyone up into the dining room to wait for the detectives.

What followed was more than an hour of interviews, during which they listened to our version of what had happened. Skeptical at first, they had no real option but to believe us. They couldn't do much else. The evidence was laying around everywhere, on the patio, in the gardens, even the pool; the grounds were littered with spent casings, bodies, blood. Dozens of spent rounds could be seen lying on the bottom of the pool.

For the next several hours the mountaintop around my home descended into chaos. Dozens of looky-loos on the road outside, jumping up and down, trying get a peek inside. The entire exterior of my home became a crime scene. The tape would stay up for days, but for now, the second Battle of Lookout Mountain was over.

Did General Grant feel as relieved 150 years ago as I did that day? I sincerely doubt it.

The police and crime scene techs tried to get us out of the house, but I was having none of it. Besides, I knew the Lookout Mountain chief, and he knew me. Better yet, he owed me. And so, reluctantly, he allowed us stay in the house; the grounds, though, were out of bounds until the techs could clear them. And that was okay by me. The gardens and pool, they could have; my home they could not.

They found three bodies. Two of them were white, one was black. I didn't know any of them. They also found two M16s, a damned AK47—can you believe that?—and a bevy of assorted hand guns. The bodies? The guy with the M16 that Bob knocked off at the pool was on the rocks below the retaining wall. They didn't find the one I got right after him. Either his buddies had hauled him away, or he'd been wearing body armor. They found the one I downed at the north end of the pool, and also the one Jacque had saved me from. That girl had hit the man with all six shots, in a group I could have covered with my closed fist, and she'd done it at night, too. I was impressed, and I made sure she knew it.

The cops ruined my beautifully landscaped gardens, climbing around all over them—that was something else the Greenes would have to pay for—removed the bodies, and confiscated our weapons. Yep, they did. It's standard procedure to remove all weapons from an active scene. I lose more weapons that way....

They also removed the bodies. There were no wounded. Well, there were, but they didn't find them. I learned later that the crime scene techs found four sites where the amount of blood on the ground suggested that at least some of the invaders had suffered serious damage.

I watched them at work under the floodlights, but I wasn't really paying attention to what they were doing. I was having a really nasty flashback. I was thinking about that twig, the one that had snapped in the dark. If they'd been more careful, if they had been just a little more experienced.... If.... I shuddered at the thought of what might have been.

It was just after two in the morning when we finally got to bed. But we didn't go right to sleep. Amanda was a bag of nerves, frightened, and in need of comfort. Which was something I was only too pleased to provide.

9

Wednesday Morning, Early

Wednesday morning broke bright and sunny, not a cloud in the sky. I got out of bed around six, showered, and then dressed for success. Nope, no suit. By success, I mean action: Peter Miller gray linen pants, white T-shirt, Gucci loafers.

I left Amanda in bed, asleep, snoring gently.

Bob and Jacque were already in the kitchen, cooking breakfast together, talking quietly. I grabbed a double-sized cup of Dark Italian Roast and took a seat at the bar.

"You all right?" I asked Jacque.

She nodded, but didn't look up from what she was doing.

"You sure?"

She glared at me, and all but snarled, "Dammit, Harry, yes. I'm fine. I only blew a hole in a man's chest big enough to drive a truck through last night. Sure thing. I'm fine. Now leave it, please."

"You also saved my life," I said quietly.

She stayed over the stove with her head down and said nothing. I looked at Bob. He shook his head, and I knew I should leave her be.

Where Rose and my dad were, I had no idea. Probably still sleeping it off.

Amanda came into the kitchen just as Jacque was serving the scrambled eggs, and Bob was handing out toast. I was already on my second cup of coffee. For the first time ever, at least since I'd known her, Amanda looked like hell. Her face was drawn, her hair was a mess, and she wore no makeup. She sat down beside me, grabbed my coffee, cradled the cup in both hands, and began slurping it down.

Who the hell is this woman?

Finally, she put the cup down—empty—slipped her arms through mine, and laid her head on my shoulder.

Who the hell cares—I love it!

The mood in the kitchen that morning was beyond somber. Jacque, I could tell, was having trouble with what she'd done, but I knew that eventually she'd realize she'd had no other choices. Would she get over it? I doubted it, but knowing her as I did... I had a feeling she'd be okay, be able to live with it. Time, so they say, is a great healer.

Amanda? No problems there, at least not in the cold light of day. She'd been under fire half a dozen times before.

And Bob? Well Bob just loves it.

No, it was my father I was worried about. He'd always known what I did for a living, and he also understood that sometimes things got a little hairy, out of hand even, but to have it rammed down his throat as it was last night.... That was way too much, and once again I shuddered when I thought of what could have happened if my instincts hadn't kicked in, if I hadn't gotten so damned lucky; if I hadn't heard that twig snap....

"I need to go find Dad," I said finally, "see if he's okay."

I found Rose still in bed. She's hadn't been awake long, but she was already crying. I could guess why. She'd probably awoken thinking about Henry, as had I several times that night.

Dad was in the bathroom. I knocked on the door. "Hey, Dad. You okay?"

"Yes, I'll be out in a minute. I need coffee. Go get me some, would you, son? Make sure Rose gets some too."

I grinned. I should have known. The old coot never let much bother him, in court or out. He was the original ice man.

I went and fetched the coffee, as he'd asked, and when I returned I found him seated on the side of the bed beside Rose, holding her hand, trying to comfort her, and what a shock I got. Never in my lifetime, not even when I was a kid, had I ever seen him in his underwear. But that was not all. The man had aged ten years overnight.

"It's okay, son," he said, catching my look. "I'm just tired. I'll get over it. How about the rest of you? How's

Jacque doing? That was a hell of a thing she did last night. I'll never forget it. Anything she ever needs, she's got it; I mean it, *anything*."

He took the coffees from me, handed one to Rose, and kept the other for himself. He glanced up at me and almost rolled his eyes. "Oh for Christ's sake, Harry, I'm all right; we're all right. Now, get the hell out of here and let me look after my wife. We'll be along shortly."

And then I did something I hadn't done in a long time. I leaned over and kissed him on his forehead. "I love you, Dad. You too, Rose." Then I left them alone, staring after me.

Back in the kitchen I grabbed another coffee, my third if you count the one Amanda had finished off, and sat down at the breakfast bar. But I was on edge, antsy, fidgety; I had to get out of there.

"I need to go prowl the gardens," I said, not to anyone in particular. "See what damage has been done. Anyone want to come with me?" Only Bob did.

We went out through the broken glass door, past the pool house to the ornamental wall, and there we stopped and looked around. Crime scene tape was stretched around the property, everywhere, and a half dozen techs were still hard at work, some scouring the patio and lawns, others picking their way through landscaped gardens down the slope beyond the pool.

"Come on," I said. "Let's go take a look down there."

I headed for the stone steps to the right of the pool that led down from the patio.

The lower gardens are one of my favorite features of

the home. There are slightly less than two acres of rock gardens, flower beds, water features, and tiny paths that meander this way and that, from side to side and top to bottom, all surrounded by a six-foot high stone wall. And now I was definitely thinking about adding some cameras, too.

"Bob," I said as we negotiated the tiny pathways, "what the hell do you think has happened to Benny? I still haven't heard from him."

"Maybe you should call him again."

I nodded. "Yeah, I think I will."

I took the phone from my pants pocket, flipped the screen to recent calls, and hit dial.

"The number you have reached is no longer in service."

Bob shrugged when I told him. "I wouldn't worry. The little pig is probably using burners."

"Yeah. Yeah, that must be it." *Jeez, I hope to hell it is.*

"Okay, Harry. What's the plan?"

We'd reached the lower perimeter wall. It was too high to see over, so we walked the half-dozen yards or so to the wrought iron gates; the lock and chain were still secure. Beyond the wall, two more techs were grubbing around in three feet of the nastiest undergrowth you could imagine. *Better them than me.*

The view was nice, but not as nice as from the patio.

"Yeah, the plan," I said thoughtfully, as we turned and began the long hike back up the slope to the house.

"I don't have one. And I won't until we find out where the hell Shady and his crew are holed up. Damn, I wish Benny would call." I looked at my watch. It was just after eight; way too early to find anyone at the Sorbonne. I would have called Laura but, hell, I didn't even know her last name. Then I had an idea.

I took the phone from my pants pocket and called Kate.

"Hello, Harry." Jeez, I could feel the ice in her voice.

Oh hell. I forgot to call her last night. "I suppose you heard."

"When did you learn to talk in understatements?" she asked. "Don't answer. Doc Sheddon has a full shop. Four bodies, thanks to you."

"Four? They only hauled three away from here."

"Yeah, I know. A dog found the extra one on the side of the mountain half a mile from your home. He was gut shot, with a .45. Your doing or Bob's?"

"Uh, mine, I think."

"What the hell happened, Harry? Did the goddamn South rise again up there or what?"

"Or what. That piece of shit lawyer, John Greene, put a contract out on me. I thought we'd handled that yesterday, but obviously we hadn't. So they came to collect the fee, I guess. Look, Kate, can we do this later? I don't have time for conversation."

"What is it you want, Harry?"

"Do you know what Laura's last name is?"

"Laura? Laura who?"

"If I knew that I wouldn't need to ask you, now would I? Benny's Laura, from the Sorbonne. I need her number."

"Oh her. Her name is Davis, Laura Davis. Hold on; I have it; I just have to find it. Okay, ready?"

She gave it to me, and I said goodbye. I wanted out of that conversation, but she was having none of it.

"Hold on," Kate said. "Don't you dare hang up on me, Harry Starke. What the hell is going on up there? I want to know—right now."

"Absolutely nothing, at least not now. Well, the techs are still mooching about, but other than that...."

"You ass. You know what I mean. What's this about a damned contract? What are you doing about Henry? Why did you want Laura's number? What the hell does any of it have to do with her, or Benny? Why are you not at work, and where the hell are Bob and Jacque? I stopped by your office yesterday and Heather was a damned clam. She wouldn't say a word."

Good for Heather. So, Kate obviously knew nothing about Shady or the Greenes.

"Wow, Kate. You have any more questions?"

"Those will do for now. Now give."

And so I did. I told her about the visit from Benny, and what he'd told me about Tree, and I told her about our visit to the Greenes. She listened in silence, and then she was silent some more, and I thought for a minute that she'd hung up. She hadn't.

"You crazy son of a bitch," she said finally. "You have Jacque involved in this mess? What the hell are you thinking? She's a secretary, for Christ's sake."

"Secretary she ain't. Not anymore. Two days ago she

might have been, but last night she saved my life. She put six in a man's chest just as he was about to nail me."

"Oh my God. I don't believe it. Is she all right? Wendy will pitch a fit."

"She'll be okay. Look, I gotta go. I need to find Benny, and fast."

"Wait! Harry, I'm in. I'm on my way up there."

"Oh hell no," I exploded. "You'll lose your damned job, or worse."

"Nope. I'm in. I'll fix it with the chief. He owes me—us—remember? Don't even think about arguing. Henry's murder is officially my case, so you have no choice. Now that we know what we know, I have cause, and I'm in, so shut the hell up. I'll be there in thirty." And she hung up.

I looked at Bob. He was grinning like a fool.

"I guess you caught most of that, right?" I asked.

He laughed. "Oooh yeah."

10

Wednesday, Mid-Morning

Bob and I negotiated the tiny pathways back to the house and found everyone still seated around the kitchen table.

Amanda was back to her normal self: dressed in shorts and a white top, wearing light makeup, her hair no longer a wild nest but back to its usual, purposely tousled look. Had I not known better....

I left Bob with them and went to the basement to what would eventually become my office. As it was, it was a somewhat sparsely furnished little room, not much more than a large closet.

I dialed Laura's number; she answered on the third ring.

"Yeah? Who is this?"

"Hey, Laura. It's me. Harry Starke."

"Oh hell. I had a feeling I'd hear from you this morning. What's up?"

"Where the hell is Benny, Laura?"

"Dunno. I heard from him earlier, about an hour ago. He wouldn't tell me where he was. He's hiding out somewhere.... Hey did you know there's a contract out on you?"

"Yes, Laura. I know that."

"They was in here last night. The bar was full of them, at least ten of 'em. Tough lookin' mothers they was too. They was talkin' about you, Harry. That's why Benny high-tailed it outa here. He told me to tell you, if you called, that he'll be in touch as soon as he knows something, that you ain't to call him, not that you can. He don't have a real phone anymore, an'—"

"Laura, Laura, stop, I got it. Did he say where he was going, who he was going to see?"

"Nope, nothin' like that. He said he'd call you, Harry, an' he will. He's a son of a bitch, an' a bit of a sloth, I know, but when he says he'll do something, he'll do it."

And that was it. I let her go. She was right. Benny was a strange little critter, but he could always be counted on to come up with the goods—if he was still alive.

When I got back to the kitchen, Kate had arrived and was at the Breville making herself a latte. She heard me come in, looked around, glared at me, and then turned back to what she was doing.

There was a Glock 26 at her waist, the holster slung over

her hips and her jeans. Her gold badge was clipped to her belt. She wore black shoes with three-inch heels that pushed her five-eleven frame up to an awe-inspiring six two.

We'd been friends and partners—and for a while more than partners—since she was a rookie cop. Now we were just good friends. We still work together sometimes though. I have a sort of semi-official standing as a consultant at the PD, both to Kate and, more recently, the chief.

"I'll have one too, please," I said, but I got no reaction, nor did I get a latte. She was in one of her moods. She finished making her own latte, then took it to the table and sat down next to Bob, which pleased him greatly.

I was beginning to think those two had a thing for each other.

I sighed, made myself another cup of Dark Italian Roast—any more of that and I'd be wired like the damned national grid—and I sat down between Amanda and Jacque.

"Talk to me, Harry," Kate said, looking across the table.

"About what? You know what happened up here last night. Besides, Rose and my father are—"

"Forget that crap," August said. "We want to know. Now answer the lady."

That was my dad, bless him. Never one to sugarcoat a situation.

"There's nothing to tell, not until I hear from Benny. I can't make plans if I don't know where those guys are. Look... oh shit." I stood up, frustrated, shoved my chair back and headed for the Breville, and tossed what was left of my coffee into the kitchen sink. I could get my own damned latte.

"Amanda, Rose," I continued, "you really don't need to be a part of this. Why don't you go out and lie by... the... oh forget it." The look Amanda was giving me would have turned a lesser man to stone; hell, even I felt a little stiff.

"Okay, you're the boss." I shook my head, beyond frustrated. "So the first thing we need do is address this contract Greene has put out on me. That means another visit to the Tower. We'll head on down there in a few minutes. Second, as soon as we hear from Benny, and we know where Tree and his gang are holed up, we move, and quickly. Another situation like we had here last night is something I'm not prepared to risk. We take it to them, and we take it fast and hard. Yeah?"

I looked around the table. Bob was nodding. Dad was holding Rose's hands between his own. Jacque's color was something I'd never seen before. Her usual caramel skin had a pasty look about it. Amanda looked both vexed and anxious. Kate? She was leaning back in her seat, one arm curled over its back, legs crossed, a half smile on her lips.

"Thoughts?" I asked.

But if they had any, they kept them to themselves.

"Kate," I said. "What are you thinking? How are you going to try to fit yourself into this mess?"

"Oh, I'm in all the way, Harry. Fully sanctioned by Chief Johnston. His final words to me when I left were, 'Try and keep his ass out of jail, and your own.'"

"Right then," I said lightly, though I didn't feel it.

"Here's what we'll do while we're waiting for Benny. Amanda, you can put Kate in the spare room at the end of the hall, but not right now.

"Kate. What weapons do you have with you?"

"Glock 26, as always. Shotgun in the car."

"Vest?"

"Yep. The Spider."

"The vest is good, but you need to ditch the Glock. I'll let you have something more appropriate. Bob, you, Jacque and me need to retool. Lookout Mountain's finest took every handgun we had in the place, except maybe Jacque's backup.

"We still have the long guns, but that's about it. So, first we'll go to the office, and then the Tower. Yeah?"

Nobody spoke. I wasn't surprised.

I nodded. "All right then. Amanda, Jacque—Jacque, you still have your 26, right?" She nodded. "Good, I want you both to stay here with Rose and my dad. We'll be back as soon as we can. Those guys won't be back during daylight, especially not with the cops still prowling about outside, so don't worry."

I thought for a minute that Jacque was going to argue, but she didn't. I think maybe she was a little relieved to be let out of this one.

I got up from the table and grabbed a lightweight navy Burberry jacket and slipped into it. Yes, it was warm outside and I didn't really need a jacket, but I did need to cover the empty shoulder rig.

"Alright, let's go."

11

Wednesday, Late Morning

We were at my offices only long enough to visit the strong room and rearm. Bob stuck with Sig 1911's, but I was having none of that; that seven-round mag had almost cost me my life. Instead I chose twin Heckler & Koch VP9s. Each held fifteen rounds, sixteen if I kept one in the chamber, which for this job I would. I handed a like VP9 to Kate, which she took, along with a custom-built holster. She also decided to hang onto her little Glock 26 and use it as a backup.

I grabbed six extra mags for the VPs, handed three to Kate, then grabbed a replacement for Jacque's Glock 19 and a full box of sub rounds. Ten minutes later we were parked at the rear of the Tower building.

I wasn't sure what we would find up on the top floor, but whatever it was, we were certainly ready for it.

As the three of us rode the elevator up, I glanced at Kate. The stoic look on her face told a story all its own. She, like me, was having flashbacks to the times we'd made the same ride together to interview Little Billy Harper, Kathryn Greene's father. I wondered what Kate was thinking. I've never had been good at reading her; she always was one of those "the less you say the better" types.

Deep down, I was glad she'd found a way to be a part of this, glad that it was her case. But I wasn't sure if her being here with me right then was such a good idea.

For the second time in two days, I slammed through Kathryn Greene's front office, hit the double doors, and marched into her inner sanctum. And there she was.

It's hard to believe this one sprang from the loins of that poisonous little bastard Billie Harper. I wonder how he's doing these days. Probably a whole lot better than he deserves.

I shoved the thoughts out of my head and concentrated on Kathryn, which wasn't at all difficult, because as soon as we entered, she stood and picked up her iPhone. Today she wore a navy pencil dress that turned her figure into a work of art. She wore her dark hair cut short in the back, but the sides were longer, layered and shaped to frame her face; she was also angry. "Livid" might have been a better word to describe her.

"You have exactly thirty seconds to get the hell out of my office. If you don't"—she waved the iPhone at me—"I'll call the police and have you arrested for trespassing."

"I am the police," Kate said quietly, pulling aside the

hem of her jacket to reveal the gold badge clipped to her belt, and the Glock 26. "My name is Lieutenant Catherine Gazzara, Major Crimes Unit. I suggest you put the phone down and sit. Where's your husband?"

That took Kathryn aback. She put the phone down on the desk, stared at Kate, then glanced at Bob, and finally she cut me a look of pure and utter evil.

Damn. Methinks the lady likes me not.

Slowly, she sank back into her leather chair, took a deep but almost imperceptible breath, straightened her back, and placed her hands together on the desk in front of her.

"I see," she said quietly. "I won't say it's nice to finally meet you, Lieutenant. My father has told me a lot about you. You're not quite what I expected. He said you were beautiful. I find you rather plain."

I almost choked, and I almost laughed, both at the same time. The lady had style, I had to give her that. Kate, however, was unfazed.

"How is Little Billy?" she asked. "Is he someone's bitch, or does he have one of his own?"

I looked across the room at Bob. I could see by the grin on his face he was thoroughly enjoying himself—as was I, I must admit.

"Touché, Lieutenant. Now, why don't you tell me why you're here?"

"I need to see your husband. Where is he?"

"He's out of town, on business. Why do you need to see him?"

"She doesn't. I do," I said. "Now where the hell is he?"

The lady was unflappable. She looked up at me in distain. "You? You, Mr. Starke? I do not have to speak to you, much less answer your questions. Indeed, I'd like to know what the hell you're doing here. You're not a sworn officer."

"I'll tell you what I'm doing here, you self-righteous.... Your piece of shit husband put out a contract on me, as you well know, and last night a small army of assassins invaded my home trying to collect on it. Four of them died. God only knows how many were wounded, and my mother and father are totally traumatized. Now you know why the hell I'm here. *So where the hell is he?*"

The change in her was dramatic. Her shoulders slumped forward; her mouth opened; her knuckles went white as she squeezed her hands together.

Hell, she didn't know. The son of a bitch didn't tell her.

She glanced warily up at Kate, then at me and said, slowly, "I'm sorry Mr. Starke, I have no idea what you're talking about."

And then I almost lost it. I stepped toward the desk, only to feel Kate's restraining hand on my arm.

"Easy, Harry," she said. "This is a lady, not one of her thugs."

"Lady, my ass. She's barely one step removed from the low lives she and her shyster husband employ. She knows damned well what contract. I was here yesterday when she told him to lift it, for Christ's sake."

"Well, be that as it may, she's hardly likely to admit to it in front of me, now is she? I could, after all, be wired."

Kate was right, but I pushed past her anyway. I leaned forward over the desk, put my hands down flat on the glass top. That put my face less than two feet from hers. She leaned back in her chair, a look of total disgust on her face.

"You tell him," I said, "that he'd better pull that contract, and now. If he doesn't, I'll jerk his balls out of his pants, stomp on them, and then feed them to him. Got it? You pick up the phone and call him, right now."

The look on her face changed yet again. The snarl was gone, replaced by an angelic smile. She leaned forward, rose from her seat, placed her hands on the table next to mine, which in turn put her face so close to mine I could smell her breath.

Minty.

And then she leaned even farther forward. For a moment I had it in my head that she was going to kiss me. She didn't. Instead, she put her lips next to my ear.

"Go. To. Hell, you arrogant bastard," she whispered. "If he has cancelled the contract, you can bet your ass that I'll reinstate it, and that I'll double the fee. I'll see you dead and in Hell, Harry Starke, and before the week is over. Sleep well you slimy son of a bitch."

And then she sat slowly down again, the same angelic smile playing across her lips.

"Was there anything else?" she asked. "If not, you know your way out."

I'm still not quite sure who won that round. I had a

sneaky feeling she might just have gotten her nose in front. Whatever. I didn't see how we could further our cause by lingering, so we left.

"So what was all that whispering about?" Bob asked, as we waited for the elevator.

"Oh, she made me a little promise," I said. "I think I may have upset her; can't think why."

At that, they both burst out laughing, and so did I, only I wasn't really laughing at all. The bitch, I was certain, meant to do exactly as she'd promised, so now I had double the number of reasons to put an end to this fiasco.

And where the hell is Benny?

12

Wednesday Afternoon, Early

It was a little after twelve thirty when we walked out of the Tower Building. I was at a loss for what to do next. I could go ferreting around Chattanooga's seamy side, looking for answers, but that would, I was sure, be a waste of both time and energy. No, there was nothing I could do but wait for Benny Hinkle to produce. But what if he didn't?

I didn't even want to entertain such a thought. He could and would get the information we needed, but the waiting was making me as antsy as a dog loaded with fleas.

I settled into the driver's seat of the Maxima and looked at my watch. It was almost twelve thirty. I took out my iPhone, checked my e-mail: nothing important. I checked my messages: same story. I sighed, and looked sideways at Kate. "Lunch, anyone?"

They both answered in the affirmative, and I hit the starter button, shoved the stick into drive, and headed south on Market Street to Warehouse Row.

"The Public House okay?" I asked, not really caring whether it was or not.

No one objected, so that was where we went. The Public House is one of my favorite places to eat in Chattanooga, but why they call it that I have no idea. It certainly bears no resemblance to its namesakes across the pond.

Fortunately the small room at the back, beyond the cooking area, was vacant, so I requested we be allowed to sit in there. It was private, quiet, and a good place to talk.

I really didn't feel like eating, but we had to do something to pass the time, and eating was better than sitting around staring at the walls.

We ordered drinks from the waiter—iced teas all round. He promised to be back forthwith, and he was. I sipped on the tea as I flipped through the menu. I don't really like ice tea, but beer or anything stronger was out of the question.

Kate ordered a burger with aged cheddar and fries.

Damn, that woman can put away the groceries, and she never puts on so much as a single pound.

Bob, bless him, ordered two burgers with cheddar—no fries.

Me? I settled for a crab cake sandwich and gribiche sauce, no fries.

We ate, for the most part, in silence. Henry's death still hung heavy over us all and I was having trouble concentrating on anything other than Benny Hinkle; he was fast becoming an obsession.

When the meal was finished, I called Amanda, made sure all was well on the mountain, and then we ordered coffee.

I could tell that Kate wanted to talk; I didn't, but what the hell.

"Harry," she said, thoughtfully, "this thing between you and the Greenes. It's personal, right?"

"Ummm, yeah. I put her dad away for fifteen years. What do you expect?"

"True, but it's more than that. I think she truly wants to see you dead."

"Which is probably why the contract wasn't lifted.... Kate, we have to squash that, whatever it takes. I don't want any more of that home invasion stuff. Somehow, we have to head the Greenes off at the pass."

"We gotta cut the head off the snake, Harry," Bob said.

What's that supposed to mean?" I asked. "Okay, okay, I know what it means, but... you're saying we kill them, the Greenes?"

"Oh hell," Kate said, getting to her feet. "I don't need to hear any of this. I'm going to the restroom. You two sort out your war before I get back."

Bob watched her go, shaking his head in admiration.

I smiled. *He really does like her*.

When he was sure she was out of earshot, he said, "Look, Harry. We've got to end this thing with Harper and his cronies once and for all. Yeah, I say we do just that: kill them. Alive, they'll come after you again and again; dead, not so much."

"Jesus, Bob. You're talking murder. Hell no. I might be a lot of things, but a murderer isn't one of them."

"It doesn't have to be murder," he said, thoughtfully. "This contract thing, that would make it self-defense, right? If we could draw them out.... Yeah, self-defense. Better yet, I'll do it for you. Shouldn't be too difficult. I could—"

"Not only no, but hell no. I let you do that, and I'd be just as guilty as you. Forget it."

"So what if I don't tell you?"

"You just did, dummy. I said forget it. You do it, I'll turn you in myself."

"Yeah right. And I believe you.... Okay, so how do you propose we do it, smartass?"

Well, he had me there. I had no earthly idea.

Soon enough, Kate returned to the table. She sat down, looked at him, then me, and said, "So what did you come up with? If it involves slaughtering the Greenes, forget it. I'll arrest you both for intent."

"We've got nothing yet," Bob said. "But, Kate," he continued, nervously.

Now there's something I've never seen before.

She tilted her head a little, narrowed her eyes, and smiled at him, but she said nothing.

"I... I've been meaning to ask you something for quite a while. Now seems as good a time as any."

Hah, here it comes.

"Okay, so ask."

"Would you... would you, umm.... Ah forget it." His face was as red as a fire truck.

She continued to look at him, but now with her head lowered, through her eyelashes; she was still smiling. He couldn't look her in the eye. Then she put him out of his misery.

"When?" she asked.

He looked up at her, sharply. "When what?"

"When would you like to go out?"

"What me? *Me?* On a date, you mean? With you? Er...."

"Jeez." She shook her head. "Yes, on a date. With me. That's what you wanted to ask me, right?'

"Well yes—that is, I um. Well... yeah."

"So the question stands. When, and more to the point, where?"

He looked at her, dumbfounded, and I knew right then that he hadn't expected her to say yes. He hadn't thought it through. I sat back in my chair, arms folded, grinning, waiting for what I was sure would come next, and I wasn't wrong.

"Tell you what, Bob," she said. "How about I take you out? My treat."

"Hell no.... No. *No!*"

"Then what?"

"I'll... I'll take you to dinner," he said, nodding enthusiastically.

"Fine. I want to go to St. John's. When?"

Now you have to understand what was going on here. We have an extremely tough, very big man—not fat, big:

245-pounds and six foot two big, a man who had just offered to kill the Greenes for me without a second thought. And we have a slender woman, lovely for sure—and yes, she was a cop and well able to take care of herself, but a woman half his size nonetheless, and he was intimidated down the tips of his toes. It was funny. You had to be there, but it was.

"When?" he all but stuttered. "Yeah, when," he asked himself. Then he heaved a huge sigh. "Not till this mess with the Greenes and Shady Tree is over. But after that, yeah?"

"Yes, then," she smiled at him, and he visibly relaxed. Then he grinned at me and winked. It was all I could do not to laugh out loud.

I pushed my chair back, left three twenties and a five on the table, and said, "Let's go home, relax, wait for the call. I've had it with being uptight about all this."

Kate left first, walking a few feet in front of Bob and I.

"Nice one, Charlie," I said in Bob's ear

"I heard that, Harry Starke," she said, without turning her head.

Bob grinned at me and nudged my elbow, the proverbial cat that had just guzzled a quart of cream.

13

Wednesday Evening

We arrived back at my home on East Brow Road at around three thirty that afternoon. All was quiet. Amanda and Jacque were poolside. My father and Rose, however, were not there. Apparently he had taken it into his head that he needed a break, to get out of the house for a while, and they had gone to the club, which was all right so long as they stayed there until I went to fetch them. Amanda had driven them over, so they had no way back, but that wouldn't stop him. He'd simply call a taxi, or prevail upon one of his many friends. I called him and told him to stay as long as he liked and to call me when he was ready to leave.

I looked around the exterior of my home and the grounds; what a damned mess. The crime scene tapes were still very much in evidence, although those closest to the house had been removed, allowing us access to the pool and patio. But the gardens were destroyed, more by the crime scene people than the invaders. I was pleased to note, however, that there was a black and white Lookout Mountain police cruiser parked discreetly at the end of the road; that made me feel a little better.

Bob had gone inside to change his clothes. I spent a few minutes with Amanda and Jacque, and then I followed him.

I changed into jeans and a golf shirt and went to the kitchen to grab a beer from the cooler. *Screw it. Just one won't hurt!*

Bob was already there in the kitchen, an incongruous bear dressed in tan cargo shorts, a white T-shirt, a white Greg Norman hat, and a pair of Jesus boots. I stopped, stared at him, and shook my head.

"What?" he asked.

"I just hope to hell you don't go out in public dressed like that."

"Meh. It suits me. That's all I care about."

"Not anymore, Bobby Boy."

"What's that supposed to mean?"

"Kate, is what it's supposed to mean."

He reddened, but didn't answer. He left and returned a couple of minutes later. The shorts had been replaced by jeans and his feet were bare. I grinned at him. He ignored me, grabbed a handful of glasses and tumblers and walked out into the sunshine.

I loaded a Yeti cooler with ice, another Blue Moon for

me—*Okay, so two is fine, right?*—a couple of Buds for Bob, two bottles of white for the ladies, and then I followed him poolside. I grabbed a lounger under an umbrella and started unpacking the drinks; Bob took another lounger and dragged it closer to the pool. He flopped down on it, beer in hand, then lay back and pulled the hat down over his eyes.

Kate was still inside. Claimed she needed a shower. *A shower before a swim? I don't think so.*

Knowing her as I did, my guess was she just needed a little time alone. I could have done with some of that myself.

"How did it go?" Amanda and Jacque asked in unison as I parked my rear on the lounger and fell back.

"Well enough, I suppose," I said, not really wanting either of them to know just how badly it *had* gone, or that our lives were still in danger.

"And?" Amanda insisted.

And she kept insisting until I laid it out for them, and by the time I'd finished they were both seated at the table under the umbrella, looking for all the world like two deer caught in the headlights of a speeding truck, which is exactly what I'd expected, and feared.

"I don't think we need to worry about another episode like the one last night," I said, but even as I said it, I wasn't sure it was true.

"They'll know we'll be on guard, and that the local police are on site, so... well, it will be okay." *I hope.*

"So what are we going to do?" Amanda asked.

I need to get Jacque out of it, I thought. *I have to do*

that. She'll be pissed, but what the hell? Better pissed at me than dead, right?

"We," I replied, "and by that I mean me, Bob, and Kate, we wait. We can't do a damned thing until we know something, until Benny calls."

"What about me?" Jacque asked quietly. "You didn't include me in the 'we.'"

"Because you aren't in it. You can stay here, with Amanda and my family, but I don't want you in any danger. For what you did last night, I'll be eternally grateful, but as far as you're concerned, it's not part of your job description, and you're not qualified, so it's over."

And then I saw the look on her face. *Oh hell, here we go.*

"The hell you say," she exploded. "Just who da hell you tink you talkin' to? I killed a man for you. I saved you ass and you wan' dump me? I don't tink so. I was in last night, and I stays in. No matter what you say."

I glared at her. She glared back. Oh, she was angry. I opened my mouth to speak, closed it again, thought for a minute. Hell, she was right. I stood up, walked around the table, took her hand, pulled her to her feet, wrapped my arms around her, and hugged her.

"Yeah, you're in," I said. "Of course you are. There'd be no 'in' if it weren't for you. I just don't want you to get hurt. You do get that, right?"

She nodded and sat down again—suitably mollified, I hoped.

Five minutes later, Kate appeared. Bob had his beer at his lips, and when he saw her he involuntary took a deep breath. Not good. The beer went up his nose and he just about choked, and no wonder. She was wearing a white, very backless one piece, and she was gorgeous. She stepped onto the springboard, performed a glorious dive, and set off for the far end of the pool at a fast crawl. Two laps in she slowed the pace, turned, and headed to the far side of the pool. When she reached it she seemed to flow up and out of the water, onto the top of the infinity wall where she lay on her back, drops of water on her body sparkling in the sunshine. A jeweled, bronzed goddess, untouchable. She was breathtaking, not in the same way Amanda was beautiful, but....

And then I happened to look at Amanda. She glared at me, and I winked at her. Bad idea. I shrugged, she rolled her eyes, and then she saw the way Bob was following Kate's every move, and she smiled, looked at me, and nodded. And life was, at least for the moment, good.

And then Benny called.

The funny thing is, I'd been waiting for the call for almost two days, and when it came it took me completely by surprise.

"Hey, Harry. It's me, Benny."

"Jeez, Benny, where the hell have you been?"

"I bin doin' what you asked, an' I bin stayin' outa trouble, an' outa sight. Harry they's lookin' for me. I cain't go home. I'm staying at one of them sleazy extended-stay, no-tell motels up here in.... Hell, never mind where. Anyway, I found 'em."

I waited for him to go on, but he didn't. I figured he

was playing for effect. Not a good time to play such games.

"Well?" I asked, in a tone of voice he couldn't mistake for anything but anger.

"They're in the Old Woolen Mill in Cleveland. You know, that big old derelict factory place on South Church, the one with the tall chimney an' all?"

"You're joking, right?" I asked. But I knew he wasn't.

"That's what I said, Harry. The Old Woolen Mill."

"You're talking about the old textile mill on Southeast Church Street."

"Yeah, that's the one. Didn' I just say that? You should pin back your ears. I cain't keep on repeatin' m'self. Now, I gotta go. Good luck, Harry."

"Hey!" I shouted. "Don't you hang up, you little creep. What you just told me is not going to get it done. I want details, dammit. Now spill."

"Harry, I gotta go. They're after me. Damn you. I never should have gotten myself involved. I'm gonna wake up dead an' buried if I ain't careful."

"Talk to me, Benny. You don't, you definitely will wake up in a coffin, only you won't be dead."

"Jeez, Harry. That's not a nice thing to tell anyone. You made my friggin' skin crawl. Ugh."

"I'll make *you* crawl if you don't get on with it. Stop screwing around."

"Look, Harry. All I knows is that Tree, Duvon James, Henry Gold, and a whole bunch of brigands are working drugs outa that mill. The tale is that they're working for Johnny the Shark—"

"Johnny the Shark? Who the hell is that?" But I already had a good guess.

"Greene! For Christ's sake, Harry, Johnny Greene, the lawyer. They's workin' for him. Shady is in charge of the troops—he don't get outa there hardly at all, on'y at night, so they say. He's like goddamn bat. Nocturnal son of a bitch, always was, but you know that...."

"For God's sake, Benny. Stop running your mouth. Forget Greene for a minute and tell me about the people Tree has working for him. How many are they?"

"They's a nasty bunch, Harry. Most of 'em is white.... Strange, that, doncha think, him bein' black an' all?"

"*Benny!*"

"Yeah, yeah, I know. I heard there was about twenny-five or so of 'em. Nobody seems to know 'xactly. As I said, they's mostly white with a few blacks an' browns thrown in. Some of 'em is ex-military—no Seals or anything, no Special Forces... well, maybe one. Some guy they call Loopy.... Maybe that's what he is, loopy.... Yeah, yeah, I know, Harry. I heard they was mostly just ex-sojers, on hard times. Couple of nasty biker types, too. Well, mor'n a couple, five or six or seven. Hey, I heard they lost a few people last night. You have anything to do with that? Don't answer that. I don't wanna know. Look, I need to get off this phone an' go somewhere safe. You'll lemme know when you've cleaned 'em up, right? You... are gonna clean them up?"

"I'm going to do my best, but I'm not done with you yet."

"Harreee. The hell you ain't."

"Benny, that's a huge building. It's vacant. Has been for twenty or thirty years. It's a death trap waiting to happen. I need to know exactly where they're holed up in there."

"I don't know that! How would I? They's in there. That's all I know. I gotta go," he said, and then he was gone.

Whew, what the hell do we do now? Twenty-five, maybe more, and bikers too, and this guy Loopy. What the hell is that about? And there are only four of us. Ah, four's a good number, and they won't be expecting us. Four to one, maybe five to one, right?

I didn't answer myself. They do say that when you start doing that, you've entered the first stage of insanity. *Yeah, and I was already beginning to wonder about that.*

I looked down at the now disconnected iPhone in my hand, leaned sideways and dropped in on the table top, picked up my glass of Blue Moon, and resumed thinking, but not for long.

"Hey," Bob said loudly. "You gonna share or what?"

"Huh? Oh. Yeah, just give me a minute. I need to get my thoughts in order. You overheard most of it anyway."

"I did."

I sipped the beer, stared at Amanda floating on an inflatable raft, then at Kate floating beside her, not really seeing either of them. I slowly shook my head. It wasn't anything to do with them. I had images of the huge edifice that was the Old Woolen Mill floating around in my head. It was going be a tough nut. That I knew for sure.

How the hell....

"Bob," I said, returning my glass to the table. "What do you know about that old mill up in Cleveland?"

"Not a damn thing. I've only been to Cleveland a couple of time. I've never even seen the place."

Well, I had, and I knew we were in trouble.

Cleveland is a small city of about forty-five thousand, give or take a couple hundred. Today it's something of a bedroom community for Chattanooga. There was a time, back in the early part of the twentieth century, when it was quite a bustling little industrial town, and the Old Woolen Mill had been an important part of it, the hub of it in fact.

I'd driven past it many times. Four stories rising eighty or ninety feet high, and spread across maybe a half dozen acres, it was an imposing and, in my opinion, beautiful old building. It was on the National Register of Historic Buildings, too. A relic of a bygone age.

But, beautiful though it may have been, if Tree and his mob really were holed up in there, it would be a nightmare in the making.

"The place is derelict," I said thoughtfully. "Huge, no electricity, no lights. It's a death trap, a damned box canyon, an ideal place for an ambush."

"So what's your plan?"

"I don't have one, not yet. We need to figure something out, though. I guess we need to do some reconnaissance. I wonder if there are any drawings, floor plans.... Nah, we don't have time to search them out even if there are. Damn, I bet it would take a week just to explore that place, and we don't have that kind of time."

"Okay," Bob said, staring at Kate over the top of his beer can, "so we go look at the place now, tonight."

"Nope. It's too late now. It's after seven thirty. By the time we got there it would be dark, and I don't want to go wandering around even just the outside of that mausoleum at night."

"Night vision?"

"No, we need to be able to build a tactical approach. We need to see what we're looking at, in daylight. I want to know the lay of the land. We'll reconnoiter the place tomorrow morning, and move in after dark tomorrow night. In the meantime, let's see what we can find on the web. Google Earth should give us an idea what we're dealing with, but we'll need better info than that. C'mon."

I got up and headed into the house. Dug my laptop out of my briefcase, opened it, turned it on and waited for it to boot up.

Bob and I sat together at the kitchen table, the laptop in front of us. We were joined moments later by the three women. They all watched as I pulled up Google Earth and then Cleveland, and then the Old Woolen Mill on Southeast Church Street.

"And there it is," I said, as I flipped from map view to 3-D, and then leaned back in my seat so everyone could see.

"Wow," Amanda said. "It's huge."

She was right. It was. Even bigger than I'd thought.

"Damn," Bob growled. "That's impossible. If they're holed up in that four-story section.... It must be a quarter mile long by 100, 120 feet wide, and look at all of those smaller buildings. And that... what's that? Looks like a slimed-over swimming pool."

"That would have been the reservoir used to feed the boilers, I think." *What the hell was I talking about? I had no idea what it was.*

"Hey, take a look at that," Kate said, leaning over Bob's shoulder and pointing at the screen. "It's some sort of canal. It looks as if it runs from beside the pool under the wall into the building. That might be a way to get inside unnoticed."

"I doubt it," I said. "But it's worth a look."

"What's this here?" Jacque asked, pointing out a strangely shaped two-story outbuilding. It was roughly a right triangle, the base of which might have been forty feet wide; the long left side maybe two hundred feet and the diagonal... hell, I couldn't even estimate it, but long.

"I don't know," I said. "This is helpful, but it's not what we need." *Jeez, Not what we need. That's an understatement.*

The five of us stared at the screen in silence for five or ten minutes more. The more I stared at it, the more impossible it seemed to be. Somewhere in that monstrosity twenty, maybe twenty-five men, had made their hideaway. Should be easy enough, right? Not hardly. I'd never been inside it, but I'd heard tales that in its heyday there had been some fifteen hundred workers in there, on four floors that had to be at least fifty-thousand square feet apiece. More than an acre per floor. I knew it must have been vast, a veritable warren, and not knowing where the twenty-five might be.... Well, you get the idea.

Finally I hit Ctrl + P to make prints of the Google Earth image. We'd need that when we went exploring the following morning.

I went to my office—okay, closet—in the basement and collected the prints, then returned to the kitchen and handed them out. When I got back, the women had left, presumably to get dressed. Bob was still staring at the image onscreen.

I joined him, sat down, snapped the computer shut, and handed him one of the prints.

"Not a whole lot of good, is it?" he asked, shaking his head as he stared at it. "How the hell do you figure on even taking a real-time look at the place? If they have people on those top floors, on lookout, we'll be spotted the minute we get there."

"Yeah, I thought about that. We'll just have to make sure we're not spotted. I think we need to go early tomorrow morning, be up there before sunup. If they are what we think they are, they'll either still be asleep, or feeling pretty secure. What do you think?"

"Makes sense. Trouble is, Shady knows you, and maybe me too. We run into him, we'll have a firefight on our hands."

I nodded. "We go, just the two of us. Kate and Jacque will stay here. They won't like it, but this is one of those times when less is more. Agreed?"

He nodded, stared at the print, shook his head, looked up at me, and said, "Harry, I have a bad feeling about this. In the dark, at night, is one thing. But in broad daylight?" Again he shook his head. "I dunno."

"That's why I say we do it early, really early. Look, sunup's around six thirty, but it starts getting light just after six. If we're there by then, and ready, we can be in and out in thirty minutes. By six thirty we can be on our way home. You agree."

"No I don't, Harry. Look at this place." He waved the print in front of my nose. "It would take us thirty minutes just to walk from one end to the other, much less *creep* around it, trying to stay out of sight. I think you're being overly optimistic."

I nodded. Looking at that massive layout, I had to agree with him. "So how would you do it?"

"That's just it," he said. "I don't know any other way that makes sense. We sure as hell can't go banging around the place in broad daylight... and that brings up another point. What about inside? The exterior isn't too difficult, but what the hell are we likely to run into inside?"

There was no answer to that. Getting inside to look around was out of the question. When the time came, we'd just have to play it by ear, and that was what I told him.

He snorted. "If that's what you think, we might as well play it all by ear. Stay here until dark and then...."

"Now you're being mulish," I said. "We leave here at five and get there before first light. That's it. You and me and your Jeep. They'll spot the Maxima before we get within a mile of the place."

He nodded.

"See here," I said, pointing at the print. "We'll come off the interstate here at Exit 20. Bear right at the red light here, onto Third Street. That will bring us to the north end of the building. We turn right here, on Church, and cruise the front of the building, turn left on Sixth, then left again on Euclid. That will bring us back to Third Street at the north end of the building. Make sense?"

He nodded.

"Now," I continued. "Look over here." Again I pointed. "See? We park right here, in this lot across the street at the corner of Church and Third," I pointed to the exact spot. "Other than this tiny section at the north end, we'll be out of sight of the entire building. We leave the Jeep, walk across the road and onto the property here."

He nodded. "Makes sense."

"I googled the Old Woolen Mill earlier," I said. "See these small buildings, the ones with the red and black roofs? They're all occupied, small businesses. As far as I can tell, those structures are attached to but separate from the main structure; there's no internal access to the main building, which means we have nothing to worry about until we reach this point here." I pointed to the spot on the image where the big chimney was located.

"At that time in the morning, the businesses will all be closed, and that means there will be no one inside.

We should be able to make our way south along the walls of those two building without any trouble. That will put us at the north end of the first four-story unit, here, and I'm betting that that unit and the one next to it will be vacant too—hell, we know they're derelict, right?"

"What makes you think there won't be anyone in them?" Bob asked.

"Well, Shady and his crew are keeping a low profile, right? So they'll stay as far away from those legitimate businesses as possible."

"Alright, that makes sense. So then what?"

"I don't know. That part we'll have to figure out when we get there. But here"—I pointed to the big triangle-shaped building—"and here"—I pointed to the gigantic structure at the far south end of the building and the single-story structure adjoining it. "In one of those buildings is where they'll be holed up. They have to be." I paused, shook my head. "Jeez, I just hope to hell they're not in that four-story monstrosity."

He leaned back on his chair, tipped it onto its back legs, and stared at photograph.

"Yeah," he said finally. "It's a plan, and at that time in the morning... it might just work."

He let his chair fall forward again, onto all four legs, got to his feet, and was about to say something when Amanda walked in, followed by Kate. Both were now dressed in jeans and sleeveless tops. Jacque followed a moment later. She was wearing cut-off jeans, a bright red halter top, and no shoes.

"You two look smug," Kate said. "What have you been up to?"

I quickly explained the plan, and was expecting all sorts of objections, but surprisingly I got none. The plan was a go.

"Okay, folks. I need to go drag Dad and Rose out of the club. Why don't you get something to eat going while I'm gone. I want to be in bed by ten tonight."

"Oh my. Lucky me," Amanda said slyly.

I grinned at her, shook my head, and headed out the front door.

14

Thursday Morning, First Light

I'd set the alarm on my iPhone for four o'clock, but when it went off I thought the Armageddon was upon us. Custer's adopted marching song "Garry Owen" reverberated around the room. *Damn, I've got to change that friggin' ring tone.*

I crawled out of bed, looked down at the beauty I hated to leave lying there, and then staggered into the bathroom and hit the shower.

Five minutes later, my nether regions wrapped in a towel, I headed down the hall to make sure Bob was up and about. He was. He was already in the kitchen, seated at the table nursing a cup of coffee.

"I made one for you," he said. "All you need to do is hit the button." And I did. "I heard that stupid tune, by the way. You need to change that."

I didn't bother to answer. I sat down opposite him,

sipped the steaming brew, looked at the clock. It was 4:25 a.m.

"It's still early, but we can head out whenever you're ready," I said.

He nodded, and I went back to the bedroom to dress. It was still pitch black outside, and would be for at least another couple of hours, but I was worried about the weather. The sky outside my bedroom window looked clear enough, but the folks at Channel 7 had forecast rain, and that was what I was hoping for, because it would provide another level of cover.

I dressed in black jeans and a black T-shirt, slipped into the shoulder rig, attached a suppressor to the VP9, checked the load—fifteen rounds—and slipped it into its holster under my left arm. The damned thing was bulky and uncomfortable with the suppressor attached, but if I ended up needing to use it, the less noise the better.

I bent over the bed and kissed the still-sleeping Amanda. She stirred, rolled over, kicked the cover off, and exposed one of the prettiest legs on the mountain.

Whew. I need to get outa here.

I donned my black leather jacket, grabbed a spare mag for the VP9 from the drawer, and stuffed it into the custom-designed pocket inside the jacket, took one last look at Amanda, and headed out to join Bob.

He was similarly dressed. We must have looked like a pair of thieves, but I was at my most comfortable dressed that way, invisible, a creature of the night.

It was almost five when Bob steered the old Jeep Grand Waggoneer through the electronic gates and out onto East Brow. The drive to Cleveland was uneventful; even I-75 was quiet, which was unusual.

We took Exit 20 onto APD 40, drove on for another mile, and then turned left onto South Lee. All was quiet as we drove past the high school. We swung right onto East Third and drove on for maybe a half mile, and there she was, on the right, a vast black shadow silhouetted against the still-dark sky.

"Turn right and go slow," I said. "No, wait. Pull into that lot over there. I'm on the wrong side. I need to be in the back."

I climbed over the seats into the back, and Bob swung the Jeep onto Church Street and we cruised slowly along the length of the building, but we were too close to see anything other than the ground floor. The interior was all in darkness; there was not a light inside anywhere that I could see. I could, however, see from the street lights and the overspill from the fire department across the road that even though there were panes of glass broken and missing, all of the ground-floor windows were secured on the inside by heavy, eight or ten-gauge steel wire mesh. Unless there was something different around back, the windows would not provide us with a point of entry, not even with bolt cutters; time would be of the essence. It wasn't an option.

We drove along the seemingly endless frontage of the building, turned left on Sixth, which was little more than a one-lane track, and slowed to a stop. The approach to the building there, at the south end, was overgrown. Two-foot-high grass fronted a sturdy wooden wall that was itself flanked by a ditch.

Hmmm, no access there either.

I tapped Bob's shoulder; he drove slowly on, then turned left onto Euclid: also useless. We were now too far from the building, maybe a hundred yards or more, and it was too dark to see anything but its outline against the barely lightening sky.

"Let's park it, Bob. Go to the end, turn left and then right into the lot, and drive to the corner of Third and Church. If I'm right, that will put us across the road from the north end of the building, and out of sight."

We found the spot: perfect. I could just see the north end of what I now figured must have been a later two-story addition. Maybe it was only one story with high ceilings. Whatever. It was home to some six or seven companies, including a wedding venue and a restaurant.

We exited the vehicle.

Hey, I thought, looking up. *It is going to rain.*

I could already feel it. Nasty for what we were about to do, but welcome, because it would provide the extra cover we needed. I caught Bob's eye over the hood of the Jeep, my eyebrows raised. He nodded, hauled the 1911 out of its holster, jacked the slide, and slid it back inside his jacket.

"Let's do it," I said. I pulled the VP9 from under my arm, racked the slide and, with my right shoulder close to the wall, led the way slowly south.

We eased our way along Bellweather Lane, a small service path that served the small business on the backside of the two-story section. No problems there. We were covered by the main wall to the right, and a five-foot-high brick wall to the left.

The end of the lane was blocked by another two-story addition. We eased to the left along the wall, then right, and found ourselves confronted by the first section of the four conjoined structures that made up the main building. I looked upward into the rapidly lightening sky. The dark wall seemed to stretch endlessly upward toward the clouds. We were on a slab of what appeared to be a fairly new concrete pad set in front of a pair of huge steel doors that must once have provided access to the interior for the service trucks. Right beside them, and just to the right, was another, pedestrian-sized steel door. Both were secured by heavy steel chains and huge locks—the small door and its steel frame had holes through which the chain was threaded. To the left and above, vast stretches of red brick were pierced by massive windows: hundreds, perhaps even thousands of small panes set in giant frames that could be measured only in yards. The ones at the lower level were maybe four or five feet above our heads, too high to see through.

"It will take a man-sized set of bolt cutters to get through these chains," Bob said as he tested the small door. It rattled; the chain held it tight. "How the hell are we going to get inside?"

I had no answer yet, so I didn't say anything. I looked along the wall to the south, and then across the dirt parking area to the east. The first glimmer of light was already upon us. We didn't have much longer.

"Come on," I whispered. "We need to get moving."

I walked quickly across the concrete pad, staying close to the wall. I didn't bother to check on Bob; I knew he would be right at my back.

South of the new concrete, and the huge chimney, was yet another office building. The concrete continued, but it was no longer new; this was the stuff of a bygone age. It was concrete for sure, but it had suffered the ravages of time: cracks had allowed water inside, which had frozen and thawed, over and over, during more than three decades of winters, reducing it to little more than rubble and dust. Vegetation had burst through the cracks, turning it into a minefield of disjointed chunks and cavities, each a potential hazard all its own, and to make matters even worse, the entire area was littered with debris—the detritus of an industry that had abandoned the building almost half a century before.

We crept onward maybe another fifty feet, then stopped and leaned against the wall, listening. Nothing.

"Looks deserted," Bob whispered. "No sign of any vehicles."

I nodded back toward the great steel doors. "I'd say they're inside. If not there, maybe at the far end. Let's keep moving. It's beginning to get light."

Sixty feet or so father on, still in the first section of the four-story building, we came to a pile of concrete blocks set against the wall under one of the great windows. Several of the panes were broken or missing. Together we climbed the blocks, stood side by side on tiptoes, and looked inside; it was dark, but there was just enough light shining in from the other side to cast a faint glow over the interior of a room. The size of it was truly staggering.

I realized then that the footprint of that room was also that of the entire section of the building outside which we stood, and that there must be three more like rooms stacked on top of it, one above the other. If this held true for the other three sections, the building contained no less than *sixteen* such rooms.

This was going to be some project. How the hell were we going to find a couple dozen people hidden among almost six acres of cathedral-sized rooms stacked four high?

I stepped down, sat down on the top layer of blocks, and looked up just in time to see Bob raise his iPhone to the broken windowpane.

"No, don't!" I hissed up at him. Too late. I cringed as the flash lit up the inside of the building.

"*Jesus Christ.* Get *down*, you ass, and stay still."

He sat. We waited. Nothing. Thank God.

"Damnit it, Bob. I hope to hell no one saw that. If they did, we're toast. No, don't say it. Let's go. We need to see the rest of this monstrosity before they catch us, if they're even here, that is."

"Sorry, Harry. I didn't think."

"It's fine. It looks like we're okay. Let's do this and get out of here.

I stood, climbed down off the blocks, and together we worked our way slowly southward along the wall.

We passed by several more steel doors, all of them

chained and padlocked. The light was coming on fast and I was becoming more and more concerned we would be seen.

A couple of minutes later, we were standing at the edge of the waterway—the pool was away to the left, unseen. I was right. At least I figured I was. It did indeed supply water to the building, but it wouldn't supply us with entry. The huge iron grill set into the wall would stop anything but a tank.

I looked at Bob and shrugged, then stepped onto a wooden plank that someone had kindly laid down as a bridge across the waterway.

We were close to midway along the third section of the wall when something made me stop, stand still, and put an arm out to stay Bob. I didn't know what it was, maybe one of those creepy feelings I sometimes got, but I listened.

I scanned the acreage in front of me, and then I listened some more. I thought I could hear water running, which was strange, because I was sure the water was cut off....

And then I saw something. Someone. I shoved Bob back into the shadows against the wall. "Look, down there. See him?"

"No, where?"

I pointed. "Right there. See that overhead door in that one-story section? He's right there, by the corner with his back to us; he's taking a leak, I think. Yeah he is. He's zipping up. See him?"

"Got him."

He was a long way away, maybe four, five hundred feet, but there was something vaguely familiar about him. The overhead door was partially open. He turned, put his hands in his pockets, looked around, walked a small circle, and then ducked under the big door. It closed behind him.

And I recognized him. It was the dreads that gave him away. Anger and hatred surged through me, white hot. I saw my kid brother strapped to a chair, that piece of garbage standing over him, that self-satisfied, arrogant smirk I knew so well on his face, and for a moment I was tempted to throw caution to the wind and charge across the open space to the door, but I knew it would have been pointless, and would only have served to give the worthless piece of crap a warning that we were onto him.

"Christ, that was Shady," I snarled. "Shit! We could have gotten him. Son of a bitch."

Bob put his hand on my shoulder, trying to calm me; I shrugged it off.

"Hey!" he whispered sharply. "Forget it. He's gone, but he's not going anywhere. Now we know they're here, and we'll be back. It's time we got out of here."

I nodded. Of course he was right. I swallowed the bile that had risen in my throat, and tried to make some sense of what we'd seen, what we now knew.

"Our biggest problem," I said, forcing myself to sound calm, "is we don't know how many he has with him. Benny said between twenty and twenty-five, but that's... well, it's not good enough. We also know that they're using that overhead door to get in and out, and that they're probably keeping their vehicles in there too. That door obviously isn't going to work for us; we have to find a way in. Come on. There's still time. Let's go look some more."

"Hey, what if he comes out again?"

"We'll hear that door and drop. C'mon. It's got to be done. We have to find a way into this mother somehow."

But the building was locked up tight. By the time we'd made it all the way to the southern end some thirty minutes later, we'd discovered nothing helpful. I was damp, pissed, depressed, and feeling like shit.

All we'd accomplished was confirming that Shady Tree was indeed in residence at the Old Woolen Mill. That, and we had a slightly better knowledge of the lay of the land. We didn't know how many men he had with him, or how they might be armed; hell, we didn't even know how to get into the place. How we were going to bust the place wide open, and hopefully put an end to the phantom menace inside the building, was something else again....

Yeah well, maybe.... I thought, then suddenly realized that, thanks to Bob, we at least had a photo of what lay inside one of those huge rooms. Or at least I hoped we did.

Hell, we have a whole lot of figuring out to do, and that's no lie.

We scrambled through the thick vegetation between the south end of the building and out onto Sixth Street, and then just stood there for a moment, wondering what to do next. We had to do *something*. It was now almost seven o'clock, and the sun was halfway up.

"Bob," I said, "you're going to have to go fetch the Jeep and then come and get me. If Shady spots me, we're screwed. We'll lose him. You can't go that way, to Third. It's too exposed. I suggest you head that way, east, then turn left on Euclid and huff it."

"Jeez, Harry. It's gotta be more than a quarter mile."

"Yes it is, so the quicker, the better. I'll wait here, out of sight."

He cut me a dirty look, and then nodded, and left for Euclid at a jog.

Me? I hunkered down among the trees like a lost chimp and waited, and waited... and waited, until finally I heard the sweet sound of that finely tuned 5.7-liter V8. I crawled out onto the road covered in bits and pieces of vegetation, twigs, and no doubt a couple nasty critters. Oh how I needed a hot shower.

"What the hell took you so long?"

"Jeez, Harry, it was a long way. I got here as quick as I could. Now for Christ's sake, get in and let's get outa here before someone spots us."

And so we did.

15

Thursday, Mid-Morning,

It was only eight o'clock; I felt like I'd been away from home for more than a week, but it was only four hours.

"Hey," I said as he turned back onto Euclid. "Take a left onto Third, then a right on Church. We'll hit Hardee's on Twenty-fifth at Exit 25. I need coffee in the worst way, and I could eat a dead dog between two loaves of bread. You know they make the world's best biscuits, right?"

He cast me a sideways, semi-disgusted look, and said, "Yeah, Harry, everybody knows that. I'll get me three-sausage egg and cheese, I think, and tots. Gotta have some tots, and maybe one of those little turnovers...."

Damn, my mouth was watering.

Less than fifteen minutes later we were on I-75, heading south back to Chattanooga, stuffing our faces with food that I, had I not known better, would have thought had been made in heaven. They really do make the best biscuits in the world. The coffee? Well, it was hot, and bitter, but it sure as hell was no Dark Italian Roast. Still, it filled the gap, and that was what I needed.

By the time we reached the Ooltewah exit, I had finished everything but the coffee; Bob was still stuffing his face with sausage, egg, and cheese. No matter. I needed to talk anyway.

"So?" I asked. "What do you think?"

"About what?" he said through a mouthful of egg. "The Old Woolen Mill? Piece of cake."

"You're kidding, right?"

"Yes, Harry. I'm kidding. The damned place is a veritable Fort Knox but without the gold. How the hell do you figure we're going to get in there? Because we've got to. Ain't no way we can bust in through the overhead door and win, and those steel doors, all of them, wow." He was shaking his head. "It's not gonna happen. We have to get in without them knowing, and we have to catch 'em with their pants down. There's only four of us, and God only knows how many of them. They see us coming, we're toast."

I didn't answer. I knew he was right. On the face of it, it looked impossible. I closed my eyes, and listened to the big tires humming on the road. Again and again I imagined the exterior of that building. I stood again on the blocks and peered in through the broken window. I'd never seen such a huge room. When we were reconnoitering the place I'd roughly paced the exterior wall of one of the sections. I'd made it to be at least sixty-five yards, so it was maybe two hundred feet long and... whew, eighty or ninety feet wide?

Jeez, that's more than half a football field.

In my mind, I made a pass down the center of the virtual room. Dozens of steel I-beams, each more than twenty feet tall and maybe two feet square, supported the even bigger steel joists that held up the floors above.

I opened my eyes. We were just passing Volkswagen Drive, heading down the hill toward Hamilton Place.

Maybe another twenty or thirty minutes and I can hit the shower, I thought, and then my thoughts drifted back to the Woolen Mill, to my nemesis in the making.

I closed my eyes, and was back in the parking lot on Third. I walked across the street and into the tiny ally—what was it called? Bellweather, that was it. Through Bellweather, around the two-story addition, across the concrete slab, past the steel doors, the concrete blocks... and then I had it. I sat up in my seat.

"Those windows, Bob," I said. "You mentioned bolt cutters for the chains on the doors, and you're right; it would take as big a set as any I've ever seen to cope with them, but the window frame...."

"Oh yeah," he said, a huge grin on his face. "They would be made of some sort of cheap, soft alloy, maybe even pot metal. It wouldn't take a whole lot to cut a section out of one of them. The blocks, the concrete blocks: they're ideal."

"Yup. You got it. We have our way in.... Wait, we do have a bolt cutter, right?"

We didn't, but ten minutes later, after a short stop at the Ace Hardware store on Lee, we did, and I was able to relax and enjoy the ride up Lookout Mountain; something I was rarely able to do. That road needs every bit of a driver's attention, especially during bad weather.

By ten o'clock we were back at the house, and I was in the best of moods. Had it not been for the shadow of Henry's death hanging over me and my family, I would have been looking forward to a wonderful day despite the rain that was now coming down in sheets.

The top of the mountain and, by default, my new home, was shrouded in mist. We were, at least for a while, among the clouds, as were the two great armies that had faced off on the mountaintop more than 150 years ago. The Battle Above the Clouds, they called it afterward. November 24, 1863.

One of these days I'm going to get one of those fancy metal detectors and take a look at Amanda's garden. Who knows what I could find?

We swept into the house to find everyone seated in the living room, gazing out at what on a clear day would have been one of Tennessee's finest views. Today the weather was foggy, raining, and quite miserable, but I wasn't, at least not then, but....

My father and Rose were in a somber mood; she'd obviously been crying, and my stomach knotted in something akin to rage. Yes, she was my stepmother, but in the years since my own mother had passed, she'd had treated me as her own. Never once had she ever used that god-awful term in front of me, to introduce me or to refer to me. You know the one, the "stepson" thing. It was something I was extremely sensitive to and, for all intents and purposes, she had been my mother for almost half my lifetime, something even I found to be a little incongruous, considering her age.

I went to the wet bar and poured myself a drink—three fingers of Laphroaig over a single ice cube. Yes, it was early, too damned early, but I needed it, and it would be the only one I would allow myself, considering the night ahead. I also made a gin and tonic for Rose. I took it her, and sat down beside her.

She turned her head toward me, accepted the drink, and gifted me with a look that was pitiful to behold. I put my arm around her, and pulled her over to kiss the top of her head. She sniffed against my shoulder, but after a moment she sat up again, gave me a wan smile, and took a large sip of her gin.

I've always been a bit of a hothead, a quick to anger, act first and think about it later sort of guy. That afternoon, though, I was experiencing something quite different. I was burning up inside and I was icy cold, both at the same time. Every time I thought about Henry, which was almost every minute, I experienced white-hot flashes of anger. I knew I needed to calm down, hence the Laphroaig, and I sure as hell tried, but it didn't help a whole lot and... well, God help Shady, or James, or whoever it was that broke my kid brother's neck. I tried to shake it off, but I couldn't, and I knew I had to. If not, if in the coming hours I let my rage get the better of me, it might well kill me.

I needed something. I looked at Amanda. She knew what was going on in my head. I could tell by the look on her face. She raised her eyebrows in question. I shook my head, turned to look out the window at the thickening fog, then took a deep breath and rose to my feet.

"You have a minute?" I asked Amanda.

She followed me down the hall to our bedroom; once we were both inside, I closed the door.

"What is it?" she asked, a questioning frown on her face.

"This." I slipped my arms around her waist and pulled her into my arms. For a long moment I held her tightly, then I kissed her, gently and with more feeling than I knew I had in me. Then I stepped away. I didn't have time for what I knew would happen next if I let it. The kiss was short and sweet, but it was what I needed. She'd always had a calming effect on me, which was what I was hoping for, and she'd never failed. Quite suddenly the black cloud over my head lifted and I felt better. I pulled her to me, kissed her again, and whispered in her ear: "Thank you."

"For what? What was that about?"

"Nothing really. I just... well, I wanted to tell you how much I love you, and that seemed as good a way as any to do it. Why, are you complaining?"

"No, sir. Not at all. It was just unexpected, that's all."

"Well, you know me. I'm the king of the unexpected."

"That, my friend, is an understatement, and oh how I sometimes wish you weren't."

"Oh come on now. You wouldn't have me any other way."

She nodded as I opened the door. "That's true, Harry," she said as she brushed past me into the hall, "but sometimes I wish.... Oh how I wish...."

She didn't need to say more. I knew exactly what she meant.

16

Thursday Afternoon, Early

After our jaunt to Cleveland, lunch was a quiet affair, something of an anticlimax. We ate our salads pretty much in silence. My head was back in Cleveland, outside that damned huge edifice, trying figure out an approach that would work.

Four of us! Just four. Not enough, but it's all we have. And if what Benny said is true, they've got maybe a couple of dozen. Five to one. Not good. Okay, so we have some planning to do.

It was going to be a long afternoon, and an even longer evening.

I looked around the table. It was a somber group, and no wonder, but we had to get to it.

"Kate, Bob, Jacque, come with me please. We'll go to the dining room." I rose to my feet and turned away from the table.

"What about us?" Amanda asked.

I shook my head. "You don't need to be a part of this. It will only mess with your head. You too, Dad." Big mistake. I should have known better.

I thought she was going to explode. "Damn it, Harry. If you think for one minute that you're going to leave me out of this, you can forget it. I need to know what's going on. I need to know what the hell you're planning," and she folded her arms, her face rigid, muscles tight.

"Me too," August said quietly.

Even Rose was nodding.

"Fine. We might as well stay here in the kitchen then, close to the coffee."

They visibly relaxed; I did not. What we had to discuss was not for the faint of heart.

"Let's go get the hardware," I said. We did, and we laid it all out across the kitchen counters. Amanda, Rose and my father stared at it, aghast. There was enough weaponry and accoutrements laid across those counters to start a small war.

I pulled up the address on Google Maps, then spread the printouts we'd made of the building out over the kitchen table so that everyone could see them, and then I began.

"Okay, so here's what we have so far, and it's not much. We figure they're holed up somewhere in this section at the south end of the building, here." I pointed to the spot on one of the prints.

"This is where we saw Shady, and round about here there's a pile of concrete blocks set against the wall under a window. All of the doors are steel and secured with heavy chains and padlocks, so we'll make our entrance through that window."

I pulled up the photo Bob had taken of the room.

"This is what we'll be getting into." They looked at the photo. It wasn't a very good one, but it was good enough to provide some insight as to the vastness of the place. The room was filled with what looked like builder's equipment—scaffolding, sections of steel forms for pouring concrete, lumber of every shape and size, some old and obviously recycled, some new; thousands of concrete blocks; bricks, wire, rebar, and a whole host of other stuff in the darker regions I was unable to identify.

"Looks busy," Bob said. "Negotiating all that in the dark will be a nightmare."

I nodded. "But there are street lamps on the west side of the building and a fire station across the street. The windows are huge, and there was light coming in from outside. I think that once our eyes get used to the low light, we should be able to see well enough to find our way around."

"I wouldn't count on it," August said. "There must be at least a dozen stairwells in there. Unless they have windows, those will be pitch black."

He was right.

But.... "I'm hoping we won't have to go to the upper floors. I'm banking on them being somewhere on the ground floor. But you're right. We have LEDs for the weapons, and some small flashlights, but we'll use them only if we have to. Anyway, from there, we'll make our way to the south end where, I hope, we'll find them. That's it. That's all I have."

"If they don't find us first," Kate grumbled quietly.

"What about outside?" Jacque asked.

"What about it?"

"You don't think that maybe they'll have someone on lookout?"

"They didn't this morning. We'll just have to hope they don't tonight, that they're confident enough not to bother."

"So your plan is to climb in through the window and wander around until you stumble onto somebody?" Amanda was angry.

"Er... no."

"Then what? That's what it sounds like to me."

I shrugged. She closed her eyes, bit her lower lip, and shook her head. I didn't answer, because I had no good answer, and because she was right: wandering around in that vast cavern of a building was precisely what we would be doing. But hell, what choice did we have? It was either that and hope that we could keep the element of surprise, or call in the local police, which I didn't want to do. I wanted Shady Tree, along with Ren and Stimpy, as I'd nicknamed Duvon James and Henry Gold two years ago, and I wanted them all to myself.

"So we take Bob's Jeep," I continued, ignoring the glare Amanda gave me, "and we leave here at midnight. That will put us in Cleveland around 12:45, give or take a few minutes. We park the Jeep here, in the lot on the north side of 282 Church Street." I pointed to a spot on

Google Maps. "It's out of sight of the mill and maybe a hundred yards from its north end."

"No," Kate said. "That's no good. If we need to get away in a hurry that's a long way to run. Here, right here." She touched the photo with the tip of her finger. "This is where we need to park, under the big tree at the north east corner, up against the wall. It will be dark, even darker under the tree."

I stared down at the photo, and then at the laptop, deep in thought. "Okay," I said, nodding. "That makes sense. Bob? Any thoughts? Jacque?"

There were none.

"Okay then. It's not much, but...."

"Call it off, Harry," August said. "You're going to get yourself and your friends killed. Call in the police. Let them do it. I don't want to lose another son."

That was exactly what I'd been afraid of when I tried to separate them from it. Damn. I sure as hell wasn't going to do as he asked, but I owed it to the others to ask.

"Bob, Kate, Jacque. How about it? You want out?"

"Before you answer that," August said. He leaned forward, put his elbows on the table and clasped his hands together in front of him. "I'd like you to tell me exactly what it is you expect to achieve. What is your objective? And please be specific."

That's my old man. Always the lawyer.

"My objective is to get my hands on Shady Tree, him and whoever else is responsible for Henry's murder."

"And do what?" he asked. "Are you looking for justice or retribution? Do you intend to kill them?"

I stared across the table at him, my teeth clamped tight together.

"Because if that's what you intend to do," he continued, "I will not allow it. I will not allow my son to commit a capital crime, no matter the reason. Harry, I *will* stop you. The minute you leave here I will call the Cleveland Police Department and tell them where you're going. I need you to give me your word that that is not your intention."

"I want them in jail," I answered. "That's my prime objective. They will, of course, resist. Someone, maybe more than one, maybe one or more of us, is likely to get hurt or killed. That's out of my control. If it happens, it happens. But I promise you I am not going up there with the express intention of killing anyone. You have my word." I meant it, too.

He nodded, and leaned back in his seat. "Good enough."

"So I'll repeat the question," I said. "Bob, Kate, Jacque, you want out?

Bob was the first to answer. "Not me."

Kate stared at me, her lips drawn tight. I thought for a moment she was going to side with my father, but very slowly she shook her head. I smiled at her.

"Jacque?"

"If you three are in, so am I."

I nodded, but said nothing. Instead, I walked out of the house and onto the patio. I sat down at one of the tables, under an umbrella. The seat was wet, but I didn't care. It was still raining, just a slight drizzle. I set my elbows on the table, my chin in my hands, and I stared out into the thick white mist.

Five minutes later I felt her hands on my shoulders. I hadn't heard her approaching. She nuzzled my ear, whispered quietly, too softly for me to understand the words, but I knew what she was doing, and I loved her for it. I put my hand on one of hers, brought it to my lips, and kissed her fingers. Then I stood and led her back into the house. The rain had begun to fall harder and I heard the rumble of thunder away to the west. If it kept up, it soon would be a storm, and I began to wonder if it was an omen, a warning. Maybe I should call it off.

No. Not a chance in hell.

17

Thursday Mid-Afternoon

When we reentered the house, Kate and Bob were sitting together at the kitchen table over coffee, heads together, talking quietly. Jacque was at the machine making a cup for herself. She looked around when we came in.

"You two want some?"

"I'll take a cup," I said.

I walked to the kitchen counter and looked at the weaponry laid out there: two Tavor semi-automatic rifles; two Heckler & Koch VP9 semi-automatic hand guns (mine); two Sig Sauer .45 model 1911s with a half dozen extended mags that held twelve rounds apiece, (Bob's); a Glock 19 and a Glock 26 (Jacque's); Kate's Glock 26, and another VP9 that I'd insisted she carry.

There was also a four-unit, Eartech wireless communication system, my expandable baton, and Bob's cut-down ball bat, four tactical vests, suppressors and extra mags for all of the weapons, and all of them, except for the two Tavors, were loaded with sub-sonic rounds, or at least they should have been. I knew mine were, but I needed to make sure everyone else's were too.

"Hey." I looked around. "What are the spare mags loaded with?"

"Subs, of course," Bob answered. "But I don't need them."

Jacque looked up from the sugar bowl, "Subs? What are subs? And why doesn't Bob need them?"

"Subsonic ammunition," I answered. "We'll be using suppressors—silencers."

She blinked at me.

"Okay, here's the short version. Most nine millimeter and smaller caliber bullets travel beyond the speed of sound. They break the sound barrier when they leave the weapon; that's why a gunshot is so loud. Suppressors muffle the noise of the exploding gasses within the weapon, but they have no effect on what happens after the bullet leaves the muzzle, on the sonic bang. So you might as well not use them. The speed of sound at sea level is 1,125 feet per second; most smaller ammo travels at speeds faster than that. Subsonic rounds are designed to travel at speeds of less than 1,000 feet per second: no sonic bang. Bob doesn't need them because he's using 230 grain .45s that travel at 850 feet per second. Subsonic."

"Ohhh-kay. Sorry I asked."

I grinned at her. "No problem my exotic, Caribbean friend. Glad to be of service."

She grinned at me, handed me the cup, then went to sit down at the table.

"And don't think it's like you see on the movies, either," Bob said. "That *phut-phut-phut* is a load of crap; it's more like a loud firecracker. Harry, have you not had her shoot one of those things?"

"I never thought she'd need to."

He rose to his feet, went to the counter, and picked up one of the Glock 19s and a suppressor. He screwed it onto the barrel and handed it to her.

"Here, check it out," he said. "Tell me what you think."

She hefted it, took a two-handed grip on it, then raised it and aimed it the kitchen clock.

"Hey," she said. "How do I aim it? The suppressor blocks the view through the sights."

He looked at me. "See?" he asked. "You should've had her fire it." He grabbed his jacket and a half dozen loaded mags, and tilted his head toward the door. "No time like the present. C'mon."

The rest of us watched them head outside. The weather had changed yet again and they took shelter under the pool house canopy from the now misting rain, not too far away from the still shattered door where we gathered to watch. In fact, they were still close enough that I could hear them talking.

Bob took the Glock from her, slammed in a mag, handed it back to her, and pointed to a small tree some thirty feet away to the right. Its trunk was maybe eight or ten inches thick. "That's your target. The trunk. Away you go."

She racked the slide, took up her stance, sighted down the barrel, then shook her head and lowered the weapon.

"I can't see anything past the suppressor. How do I do it?"

"Line of sight and instinct," Bob answered. "Try it."

She fired five shots. What little noise they made was lost in the swirling mist and drizzle. She missed all five times. Afterward she lowered the weapon and looked sideways at Bob, frustrated.

"Show me," she said, handing him the Glock.

And he did. He didn't bother with a two-handed grip. He snapped five shots off as quick as he could pull the trigger, and then handed it back to her. Every one of them was a hit. And not only that; even from where I was standing I could see that the group was tight, no more than six or seven inches or so in diameter.

She stood open-mouthed. "How did you do that?"

"Here, give me the weapon. Good. Now Point at the tree with your finger. Yes, like that. Don't try to be precise. Let your instincts take over. Like this." He swung the weapon quickly and snapped off another shot. Bark flew of the little tree trunk.

"Here." He handed the Glock back to her. "Try again. Don't try to sight it. Point and look over the top... no, both eyes open. Squeeze."

She fired the final four rounds in the mag. Two of them missed, but two clipped the trunk.

"Yes!"

"Good. Now do it again."

And she did. She wasn't great, but by the time she'd emptied the sixth mag, she was hitting the tree one time out of three.

"You know," Bob said, as he came back into the house, "if those suckers are wearing vests, these subs will bounce off them like peas."

"I know, but what's the alternative?"

He shrugged. There was no alternative.

I looked toward Jacque. She was at the kitchen counter reloading the empty mags, then I looked at the kitchen clock. It was after five. *Sheesh, still seven more hours.*

And the time dragged, and dragged, and.... By nine o'clock I was getting really antsy. August and Rose had retired early; Rose was still a mess, and I wasn't feeling too chipper myself.

I couldn't even have a drink. If we got picked up with a car full of firearms and drink on our breaths—well, you can imagine, right?

I couldn't eat, either. My guts were in knots. Scared? Not hardly. Was I worried? Hell yes I was. I was worried my friends were going to get hurt, or worse. Fearful? You bet. I'd learned a long time ago that a healthy dose of fear could keep you alive. Idiots who know no fear tend to be the first to die. But I don't think it was fear that was playing hell with my gut. I think it was anticipation.

By ten o'clock I was sitting outside, under the canopy, listening to the rain and drinking what must have been my tenth cup of coffee. I was wired, tight as a damned drum and antsy as a Jack Russell terrier on steroids.

Speaking of Jack Russells, I wonder how Merry's getting along at the farm. Merry is.... Nah, that's a whole 'nother story.

I tossed what was left of the coffee out into the rain. *I gotta quit drinking this stuff while I still can; I'll be up all night. Wait, what the hell am I thinking. I am going to be up all night.* I grinned at the thought, got up from my seat, and walked through the rain back into the house.

By eleven thirty I had calmed down and changed into my gear: black jeans, black T-shirt, black Lowa Renegade boots. The time was just about upon us and I felt... excited? No. I was calm, at peace. I was ready.

18

Thursday Evening, Late

They were all waiting for me in the kitchen. Amanda was seated at the table. She was pale, but there was no sign of anxiety on her face. There was no sign of August and Rose, either.

Both Kate and Jacque wore black North Face Isotherm tights and tops. Bob was also in black, and already in his tactical vest.

"Let's get kitted up," I told them.

I went to the counter, and was joined there by Kate and Jacque; Bob remained seated at the table.

I picked up one of the Tavor semi-auto rifles, hefted it. It was short, even stubby compared to an AR. I fitted one of the over-the-barrel suppressors to it, and nodded—the profile of the gun was little changed. I set it down, donned my vest, and then fastened the lightweight utility belt around my waist. I attached six-inch suppressors and

Surefire LED laser sights to my two VP9s and slid them into their holsters. Not quite as comfortable as I would have liked, but it would have to do. Finally, I grabbed a couple handfuls of plastic cable ties and stuffed them into my jeans pocket.

Kate and Jacque went through the same routine. We all had belt and ankle holsters. We each had two double-magazine holsters on our belts, one on each hip. These we filled with spare mags. Kate clipped her badge to her belt. She looked up and caught me looking at her.

She shrugged. "Can't hurt, can it? And if we run into the locals, it might do us some good."

Finally, I handed out the wireless communicators, clipped my Talon baton to my belt, slid a small Maglite into one pocket of the vest and a unit of Freeze+P into another. I was as bulked up as a body builder after a month on steroids.

I turned from the counter, leaned back against it, crossed my ankles, folded my arms—not an easy task over all the hardware—and looked at Bob, who was still sitting at the table.

He grinned at me. "What the hell do you think you look like?" he asked. "You look like friggin' Rambo. And the two Charlie's Angels.... Well, you both look lovely; there's no denying that."

I glanced sideways at them. He was right about both of them, even in tactical vests. "Are you coming, Donatello?" I asked him. "Or have you decided to stay here?"

He gave me one of those "are you kidding me" looks, and said, "I'm coming, I guess."

He stood up, stretched, yawned, and then proceeded to load himself up. By the time he was done, he had little room to talk about the way I looked; Bruce Willis would have been proud of him.

"You sure about no night vision?" he asked.

I nodded. "Too bulky, and if we're surprised they could be more trouble than they're worth. Once we're inside, I think we'll be fine. The streetlights will help, at least on the ground floor. We'll take Maglites to use in the stairwells and other dark areas."

He nodded. "Makes sense."

"Okay," I said quietly. "This is it, people. We, just the four of us, are it. No matter what, I will not call for outside help, not even the local cops. I don't want to get anyone killed. So...." I looked around, at each in turn, ending with Jacque. "This is your last chance to pull out. Jacque?"

She shook her head, her lips a tight, thin line.

I looked at Bob and Kate; both shook their heads.

"All right then," I said. "Let's do this."

They nodded, and then trooped out to the garage, leaving me with Amanda.

She stood, took two steps forward, wrapped her arms around my neck, kissed me, pushed me away, and said, "Be careful."

I nodded, brushed her lips lightly with mine, then said, "Bye. See you later."

"You'd better."

19

Friday Morning, Very Early

The drive to Cleveland was uneventful, and uncomfortable.

It was almost one thirty when we arrived at the junction of South Lee and Third. The streets were deserted. It was raining just enough to keep the windshield wipers running.

I was already antsy. We needed to get off the streets. If we got stopped there'd be hell to pay, and I didn't breathe easy until Bob turned off the Jeep's lights and swung into the parking lot at the Old Woolen Mill. Two seconds later we were safely tucked away under the big tree, close to a wall of the building, and inwardly I heaved a sigh of relief.

Bob rolled the windows part way down, turned off the engine, and we sat quietly—listening, and waiting to see if we'd been spotted. We hadn't been, and under the tree, in the dark the way we were, it was unlikely that we would be. Still, I figured it couldn't hurt to wait and see, at least for a few minutes. It wasn't as though we had an appointment.

"Okay, people. Ears on and test...." One by one we spoke into the Eartech system. All was in order. "Good. Do not turn them off under any circumstances, and when I call for you to check in, respond immediately."

Somehow, under all the gear I was wearing, I managed to twist in the seat and face the two women in the back.

"Ready?" I asked. They both nodded. "We'll be going in blind, so stay close and tread carefully. The exterior is a minefield of junk and debris."

I looked out of the car window. It was one miserable night. From where we were, the visibility at the rear of the building was next to nothing. There were a couple lamps on the north end, but beyond that, all was blackness.

I opened the car door, stepped out, slipped the strap of the Tavor over my shoulder and let the weapon hand hang loosely in front of me. I put my back against the wall and listened. Nothing. I nodded at the car. The doors opened, and they joined me one by one.

I slung the Tavor over my shoulder, pulled one of the VP9s. I didn't need to rack it. It was loaded with sixteen rounds.

"This way," I said, leading the way east to the end of the building. I peeked around the corner—nothing—and then slid sideways onto Bellweather Lane.

It was slow going. The lights on Bellweather led us only a few yards before we were once again engulfed by almost total darkness.

For what seemed like an hour, we worked our way south along the rear of the building. Bellweather gave way to the two-story addition, which we circumnavigated with little difficulty, and then we were at the big steels doors.

"The window is maybe fifteen or twenty yards that way," I said. "Gimme the bolt cutters." I waited, but no one said a word.

"Well?" I hissed.

"I left the damn things in the car," Bob growled.

"Holy Mary—go get 'em, for Christ's sake." And he did, and we waited, trying to shelter from rain in the lee of the steel door. Fortunately, we didn't have to wait long.

"Here you go," he said, seemingly not the slightest bit perturbed.

I snatched them from him, and immediately regretted my impatience.

"Calm down, Harry," he said. "We're cool. There's no one around."

"You don't know that," Kate hissed. "Harry, I don't like this. If they're here, they're bound to have people on watch; I would, and I know you would, and my recollection of Shady is that he's nobody's fool. Hell, he might even have cameras installed."

Yeah, I thought. *She's right. And they've done wonders with night vision technology lately. Oh well, there's nothing we can do about that now. If he does have lookouts, or cameras, they already have us. If not....*

"There's nothing we can do about it now. We either go ahead or we quit. You can do as you like, but I'm not quitting."

I holstered the VP9, shoved the Tavor to my back, shouldered the cutters, and continued working my way along the wall to where we'd found the pile of blocks.

We must have gone ten yards beyond where the blocks should have been before I realized they were missing.

My blood ran cold. I stopped dead, whirling around to double check. Yep, they were gone. And that could mean only one thing. Someone had seen us.

"Shit," I said. "They're expecting us. Back up guys. Back up."

A couple of minutes later we were back on the concrete pad outside the steel doors, our backs jammed against the brickwork.

"Now what?" Jacque asked. She sounded calm. Inwardly, I smiled.

Funny how, when people come under extreme stress, their whole psyches change to cope with the situation. This girl is doing okay.

"Okay," Bob said. "There's no way we can reach that window without something to climb on, and if they know we're here, they're probably lying in wait for us inside. So what do we do now?"

Right at that moment, I had no idea. This was no movie; it was real life.

"Just hold still for a minute," I said. "Let me think, and listen."

And listen I did, but all was quiet. The rain had stopped. Only the soft *drip, drip* of droplets falling from the rusted gutters almost a hundred feet above our heads disturbed the stillness. I glanced down the side of the building, to where the concrete blocks had once provided access to the huge window, but it was too dark to make anything out.

Like Bob had said: we would not be going through that window. I looked to my left, at the lock and chain that secured the pedestrian door.

Jesus, those links must be a half-inch thick....

"Here," Bob whispered. "Gimme those cutters."

"What for? You'll never get through that chain."

"Wanna bet? Forget the chain."

I handed them to him. He opened them and set them on the hasp of the lock. I shook my head. The lock was old—hell, it looked like it had come with building—but it was big, and the hasp was almost as thick as the chain.

No way.

He took a deep breath, and then another, and then he applied force. His biceps bulged under the vest; he put his head back, closed his eyes, gritted his teeth and, with a snarl a tiger would have been proud of, he strained and—

Bang! The hasp gave with a crack like a rifle shot. He dropped the cutters, drew one of his Sigs, and dropped to one knee, searching the blackness for any sign that someone had heard the lock break. I stepped back against the wall, and so did the women, and we waited, holding our breath, listening: nothing.

"Jesus H. Christ," Bob whispered. "That was a tough f—"

"Yeah," I said, "now shut up. Don't move. Stay still and stay quiet. If they heard that, they'll let us know."

We waited at least five minutes, and finally I said, "Okay. Good job, Bob. Let's see what we've got."

Bob grabbed the chain and hauled it, rattling and clanking like Marley's Ghost, through the holes in the door and frame. Once he'd tossed it aside, he turned the big brass knob—fortunately, the door wasn't locked. The key had probably been lost long ago. It opened with a whisper; another bad sign. Someone must have been oiling the hinges.

We stood for a moment, listening; still nothing, so I stepped through the opening into blackness. I turned on the Surefire LED on the VP and swept the beam back and forth. We were in a huge, sunken area, a loading dock or vehicle well maybe five or six feet below the main floor level, which extended some fifty or sixty distance beyond.

There were four vehicles parked in the well: a black Mercedes C-class sedan, a black Mercedes SUV, a white Lexus SUV, and a Ford Expedition. They were here all right.

I looked at Bob and gestured toward the vehicles. He nodded.

There were steps at the far end of the well that led up to the main floor and a small access door, also closed.

I hope to hell that's not locked.

It wasn't. I pushed it open gently, then stepped back and listened. There was an unearthly stillness about the place. Beyond the door I could see light; it was dim, but maybe it would be enough. I turned off the Surefire, holstered the weapon, unslung the Tavor, and operated the action. I cringed as the sound of the bolt snapping into place echoed off the walls. *Jeez.*

"Stay close," I whispered, "and keep your ears open. I don't like this. I'm almost sure they know we're here. If not, they sure as hell must be expecting us."

I squeezed through the half open door and, keeping my back to the wall, moved left. I went just far enough to let the others in behind me, then stopped and looked around. What I saw took my breath away.

We were at the northern edge of an enormous room. From the outside looking in, it had been big. From the inside, it was vast: at least two hundred feet long and maybe half that wide. The east and west walls were pierced by huge windows. Those to the west were aglow, giant church windows lit up by the street lamps and the fire station beyond, beams of amber light filling the room with a dim, unearthly light, turning it into a nightmare world of light and shadow that stretched away into nothingness. Huge steel supports stood like Emperor Qin's terra-cotta army; they too cast giant shadows. And as far as the eye could see, row after row, stack upon stack of building materials and equipment stretched away into the distance. I looked up and down the rows between the supports, trying to decide on a plan.

I inched my way along the wall and peered around

the end of it. The southern wall of the loading dock stretched all the way to east wall—the windows on that side of the building were dark.

"Kate, Jacque, go left. Take the east side, and stay in the shadows. Bob, you take the west side. I'll go down the center. Keep your ears on and live. We'll meet at the far end. If you hear anything, anything at all, take cover and spread the word. Okay?"

They nodded.

"Let's move."

We separated, but for a moment I stayed where I was and watched as they headed out. When I was sure they were all safe and in position, I moved out between the stacks of building materials.

The stillness was overpowering. Every once in a while, I heard a vehicle pass on the street outside, but that was all. The car headlights swung shadows across the room. I moved forward with the Tavor across my chest, listening for even the slightest sound that might indicate we were walking into an ambush.

When I reached the double wooden doors at the south end of the room, Bob was already there, leaning against the wall like some itinerant worker, waiting.

"Took your time," he said. "Where are Kate and Jacque?"

They arrived before I could answer. The double doors stood open a little, wide enough for us to make it through in single file, which we did. On the other side we found ourselves at the bottom of what once had been a service elevator. It was obviously a sad remnant of what it had been. The elevator cage itself lay in pieces at the bottom of the shaft, a heap of tangled, rotting wood and rusting wire. The wire mesh doors lay broken in front of it, the gears and cables that had once hauled it up and down the four floors were lying in a tangled heap atop the pile. To the right a wide flight of wooden stairs led upward around the shaft.

I looked at the stairs, then at Bob. He shrugged. I stepped past the elevator to the double doors beyond. These opened up into another great room, a twin to the first one, and I had no doubt that there were two more just like it beyond that one.

"What now?" Jacque asked.

Good question. I wish I had a good answer.

I looked down the length of the second room; it too was packed with building materials.

Someone must be using the place as a warehouse.

I stepped back to the foot of the stairs and peered up into the darkness.

"We have a problem," I whispered. "I have one of those weird feelings." And I did. For the last several minutes my skin had been crawling.

I looked at Kate. In the dim light I could see the worried look on her face.

"We're being watched, aren't we," she said.

"I don't know. I just feel.... I dunno, maybe."

"So what are we going to do?" Jacque asked.

I had no answer. This was a first for me too. I had no SWAT team at my disposal, and what little urban warfare training I'd had had been with the PD, and it was nothing compared to this. Hell, I was worried—worried we were walking into a trap, worried the people I cared about were putting themselves in deadly danger... and I was worried for myself. But those were problems I didn't dare dwell on. I had to figure out what to do, and quick.

Mentally I shook out the cobwebs, and made a decision.

"Bob, you and I will take the high road, see what's on the upper floors. Kate, Jacque, you stay down here and watch our backs. Keep an eye on the rooms fore and aft. If you see anything, holler, okay?"

They both nodded. I twitched my head at Bob and started up the stairs. Two turns around the elevator shaft and we were on the second floor, where we found two more rooms, north and south, each identical to the ones below except that these were swept clean, and the light from the street streamed in unrestricted. A million dust motes floated in the golden beams of light.

No steel supports up here, or steel joists. Everything here was made of wood, and massive.

They built them to last in those days. And these wooden floors would make some nice furniture.... Hell, Harry, stick to damned task at hand.

It was then that we heard the commotion downstairs, a whole lot of yelling and shouting, but no shooting.

What the hell?

I ran to the stairs, tripped over a loose board, and almost fell headlong into the open shaft. I caught hold of a wooden support and managed to save myself. Bob ran past as I dragged myself out of the hole. I rolled over onto my back, pushed myself up and onto my feet, and ran down the stairs after him. I found him at the bottom of the stairwell on one knee beside Kate, who was flat on her back, struggling to sit up, blood streaming from a cut on her forehead. A man lay facedown, either dead or unconscious, in the doorway. Of Jacque there was no sign; she was gone.

Bob dragged Kate into sitting position. I turned on my Maglite; she looked like hell. There was a deep cut on the right side of her forehead, and a long graze on her cheek.

"What the hell happened?" I asked. "And where the hell is Jacque?"

"She's gone. They got her. They took us by surprise. They grabbed—"

"Oh shit, no," I dropped my ass on one of the stair treads and put my head in my hands. "No, no, no! *No!* How the hell…?"

She looked angrily at me, grabbed Bob's arm, and hauled herself onto her feet.

"We were taken by surprise. And don't you look at me like that, Harry Starke. They were behind us, came at us out of nowhere at a run, out of that damned mausoleum we'd just come through. They blinded us with flashlights. We—no *I* wasn't looking in that direction. There were four of them. They were after both of us, I'm sure. Two of them grabbed Jacque and rushed her away through there." She waved her hand in the direction of the second room. "The other two came after me." She glared at me and then at Bob.

"I kicked one of them in the balls and downed him. He dropped his flashlight and ran his head into the doorframe; his flashlight is over there." She pointed. It was lying by the elevator shaft.

"His name is Loopy, by the way. When he saw him go down, the other guy yelled his name, then came at me. He got me in the head with a damned huge Maglite, and I went over backwards. I thought he was coming for me, but he must have heard you guys coming down the stairs.... What was that God-awful crash I heard?"

I shook my head. "That was me. I decided to take the elevator."

I know, I know. It was no time for joking. But it times of extreme stress, that kind of crap seemed to flood into my head.

"They've got Jacque, then?" I asked. "Oh shit.... Did you recognize any of them?"

She shook her head.

"Okay," I said. "Let's not panic. We need to think this through. Bob, see if that one's still alive. If he is, strap him up."

"Yeah, he's still breathing." He jerked the man's hands behind his back and fastened his wrists together with a nylon cable tie.

"We should have stuck together," I told Kate. "Christ, I knew something was going to go wrong. I could feel it. Now we really are in the crap. They've got Jacque, and any advantage we might have had is gone. So what the hell do we do now?"

I sat down again on the bottom step of the stairs to think.

Christ, the son of a bitch has us. Worse, he has Jacque. Damn! Damn! Damn!

"Hey, Harry. Harry Starke. You there?" The words echoed through the building. All three of us froze. "I know it's you out there. This is your old buddy, Lester Tree, but you knew that, didn't you, Harry?"

"As soon as Duvon broke that boy's neck I knew you'd be comin', just a matter of time. I told 'em so. I sure as hell did. An' you, you must be crazy, man. You thought you'd be able to take me by surprise. Hell, I had you pegged the minute you parked that piece of shit Jeep early this morning. I was surprised it took you so long. I had Duvon up on the water tower. He spotted you right away. You need to come on out now, Harry. I have a friend of yours here, a pretty little Caribbean girl. You don't come out right now, Henry here will cut her throat."

I looked at Kate and then at Bob, and then I got to my feet and went to the door. I looked down the vast stretch of the room, but I could see nothing.

"Shady," I shouted. "Turn her loose unharmed and you'll get to walk out of here."

His laughter reverberated off the high ceilings. "Harry, you're so full of crap. Hey, I told you, give it up or kiss your little coffee-colored lady's ass goodbye... well, before Duvon does. Pretty little thing, she is. Hell, she's not so little, either. Jeez, I bet she's hot. She hot, Harry?"

"You son of a bitch, Tree. You lay so much as a finger on her and—"

"And you'll do what? What you gonna do, Starke? You have any idea how many people I have with me? Eighteen. I have eighteen. How the hell many you got? Six? I have you outnumbered three to one...."

Hah, I could almost hear him counting it out on his fingers.

"Yeah, that's right, three to one!" he shouted. "I got the numbers an' I got your little Jamaican bitch. So your ass, Harry Starke, is all mine."

I looked at Kate, then at Bob. "Eighteen," I whispered, less this one," I nodded at the prone gunman. "And he thinks we're more than we are."

"That makes no difference at all," Kate said. "Not if he has Jacque."

"Harry? You still there? Talk to me boy."

"Yeah, Shady. I'm still here."

"You wanna know how we knew you were comin'? One of my guys spotted the flash when you took a picture through the winder. I even gave you a chance at me. I went outside and took a leak. I spotted you, Harry. Damn you though. You didn't take the bait. You always was a savvy son of a bitch. We would have had you then if you had. Never mind, though. You're here now, right?"

He paused, laughing, and then continued. "Okay, Starke. This is how we're going to play it. You're going to put down your weapons and you're going to walk toward us with your hands high in the air—"

The crack from Bob's suppressed Tavor reverberated

through the room. It was followed by at least a dozen more as he fired as fast as he could pull the trigger.

"Jesus Christ, Starke. What the hell are doin' shootin' at me? Didn't I just tell you I got your bitch? I'll kill her ass you don't do as I say—"

Again Bob interrupted him, emptying the magazine at the dark shadows at the far end of the room.

"Bob!" Kate yelled. "Stop. He'll kill her."

"No he won't," Bob said, ramming a new mag into the rifle. "She's too valuable to him."

"Bob's right," I said. "Tree needs her to get to me. He won't kill her. Not until he has no other option. If we get to her first.... Come on! Kate, you go left; Bob, go right. I'll take the middle. Quick now, on my mark."

"Starke you f—"

I unloosed a hail of fire from my own Tavor. I emptied the mag, all thirty rounds, tossed the gun to one side, dragged one of the VPs out of its holster, turned on the Surefire LED and the laser, and yelled, "Now!"

I charged down the middle of the room at a run, heading for the darkest area, where I figured he was, and was greeted by a hail of suppressed fire from the shadows at the southeastern corner of the room.

Most of the slugs howled over my head, slamming into the stacks of building material. I heard Bob and Kate follow me into the room and head their separate ways, but I knew they were no use to me now. I was on my own. I heard the heavy crack of Bob's 1911, and I dropped down behind a pile of pallets.

I saw muzzle flashes in the dark, and for microseconds the room was in daylight, and the gunshots echoed.

So, some of them don't have suppressors.

I snapped off two shots in their direction, heard a yell, jumped to my feet, ran three paces more, dropped again. Fired three more into the shadows and was rewarded with another yell.

In the meantime, I could hear the suppressed fire from Kate's Glock. She was moving quickly along the east wall, firing as she went. Then Bob opened up. He snapped three quick shots from the west wall. If they hit anything or not, I had no idea. What I did know was that we had taken back the advantage, at least for a little while. Now all we had to do was keep it.

That's the singular advantage of a suppressed weapon. The enemy has no idea where the shots are coming from, and that's extremely disorientating.

I jumped to my feet and ran toward the far end of the room. I hit the wall, dropped the empty mag out of VP and slammed in a replacement, racked one into the chamber, turned the Surefire off, then dragged the second VP from its holster. And then I was up and running again, heading for the big doors.

Without stopping, I charged on through the double doors, took a sharp left and ran along the wall, then turned left again into another darkened stairwell. I'd guessed right. There were five of them, plus two more wounded, and they weren't expecting me. They were all facing north, toward Kate, who was hurling a steady stream of suppressed fire toward them. I could hear the muted fire of her Glock as she moved steadily forward.

I fired twice, into the wall above their heads, and yelled, "Drop 'em! Throw 'em down! Now! Facedown—lie facedown! Get your hands where I can see 'em. Do it now, or I'll blow your goddamn heads off!"

I had taken them completely by surprise. They turned toward me, wild-eyed, and slowly raised their hands, their weapons clattering onto the concrete floor, dropped to their knees, and then lay face down, their hands outstretched in front of them. I holstered one of the VPs, turned on the Surefire on the other, and lit up the murky stairwell.

Kate burst through the opening, Glock poised, and began systematically kicking their weapons out of reach. That done, she holstered her Glock and, while I watched them, proceeded to strap their hands behind their backs with electrical ties.

So we had one tied up back at the elevator, and five more tied up here along with two wounded; one had been creased along the left side of his head. I turned the Surefire on him. The bullet had gouged a five-inch furrow through his scalp just above his right ear. It must have clipped the skull, because I could see the bone, and he was in a heap in the corner, unconscious and bleeding steadily. The other I wasn't sure about. I couldn't tell if he was gut-shot or not. For sure he had a hole in his left side just above his hip, and he was on his back, nursing it, blood running through his fingers, and moaning loudly. But would he live through it? God only knew.

Kate had also put two down fifty feet away to the north by the east window. That made ten, more than half of Shady's army and, surprisingly, no one was dead yet. *But where the hell is Bob?*

"You crazy bastard," Tree yelled, from somewhere way at the south end of the third room. "I'm gonna kill the bitch. You hear? I'm gonna kill her ass sure as hell if you don't throw your shit down an' come out with your hands up."

Crack, crack, crack! Crack, crack, crack! Six shots from Bob's suppressed .45 hammered into the shadows, where we now knew Tree must be hiding. They were immediately followed by a scream. Bob was down at the south end of the third room. He fired again, and three more slugs hammered into the shadows: another yelp echoed out into the room. Shady was bleeding soldiers fast. He'd just lost at least two more. You don't get hit with a .45 and stay on your feet.

"Damn, damn, damn, damn you, you bastards!" Tree screamed it at the top of his lungs. I could almost see him jumping up and down with rage. If the situation hadn't been so dire, it would have been funny. It wasn't. That crazy son of a bitch was within an ace of killing Jacque.

"Starke, you—"

Crack, crack, crack! This time it was me who cut him off as I ran south, head down, between the stacks of loaded pallets, Kate close behind me. I reached the far end of the third section of the building and stopped.

"*Shit!*" Tree yelled. Then all was quiet.

By now all three of us were at the southern end of the

room, Kate and I to the left of the big doors, Bob to the right, with, our backs to the wall.

"Okay, Starke. This is your last chance." Tree's voice was calm now. He'd obviously gotten a hold of himself.

"One more shot, just one more, you son of a bitch, and she dies. No foolin'. Henry will cut her neck and then hang her upside down to drain. So, you gonna quit, or what? Here, you want some help decidin'?"

Jacque screamed, long and loud.

I shook my head. I believed him. This was it. I looked at Kate and nodded.

"You win, Shady. Bob, no more. Stand down."

"What?" Tree yelled. "Bob? You? What about the others?"

I looked at Kate, tilted my head, questioning. She gritted her teeth and nodded.

"What others?" I shouted. "We're it, Shady. Just the two of us."

"You piece of shit, Starke. You took out thirteen of my men, just the two of you?"

"Yup, just the two of us." I turned to Kate and said, quietly, "I wonder if he's counting the one at the elevator shaft?"

She gave me a funny look, but didn't answer.

"If he isn't, that's fourteen. That means he has only three or four left: Duvon and Gold, maybe two more, plus himself. I like those odds, especially since he doesn't know about you."

I pointed at her, and then tapped one of my Eartechs. She nodded. I gestured for her to back away to the east wall and take cover. She nodded again, then turned and ran silently away into the darkness. That left me on the east side of the opening, Bob on the west.

I leaned sideways and peered through the wide-open double doors. The room beyond was unlike the other three. It wasn't quite as big, but the ceiling was at least twenty feet higher. There was a row of what I took to be small offices high up on the east wall, thirty or more feet above the floor, with a narrow steel catwalk running in front of them.

Observation platform?

The room was clear—no building supplies, nothing; just a vast concrete pad, a wide open space.

The lights from outside the west windows lit what few upright supports there were and cast long shadows across the concrete. It was darker, but not so dark I couldn't see Jacque seated in one of a half dozen steel chairs. She was facing us. Her hands were tied behind her, but I couldn't tell if she was also tied to the chair or not. But what bothered me most was that Shady was nowhere to be seen—and that Jacque was flanked by Duvon James and Henry Gold. Gold was behind her, holding the biggest goddam knife I've ever seen to her throat, and he was grinning.

Where the hell is Tree?

I looked up at the catwalk. There were lights on in the two center offices, and I could hear a generator running quietly somewhere off to the southeast. A small door at ground level led off into what I assumed must be the room with the overhead door where we had spotted

Shady relieving himself. And there were dark areas in both corners that I assumed were stairwells. But there was no sign of Shady.

I turned my attention back to Jacque and Gold. He was behind her, but I could see most of his head; only his chin was hidden below her shoulder. I calculated the distance. I made it roughly seventy-five feet. In this low light, it would be a hell of a shot.

"What are you thinking, Harry?" Bob whispered across the opening.

"I'm thinking I can make the shot."

"Harry. You miss, she's dead either way: your bullet or the knife."

I nodded. "*If* I miss, which I won't. Look, they won't be expecting it. Shock and awe, right? The only problem I see is Shady, but where the hell is he?"

There was still no sign of him.

"So." I looked at Bob. "You take Duvon, I'll take Gold. Wait 'till I shoot. We don't want Gold accidentally slicing her head off. I'll take a step sideways and take out Gold. You ready?'

He nodded. I took a deep breath, stepped quickly to my right, dropped to one knee, and fired; Bob fired a split second later. I hit Gold slightly to the left of center, high on his right cheekbone. His head twisted to the right. The hollow point virtually exploded as it hit, showering both Jacque and Duvon with blood and bone. The knife dropped from his hand and Jacque leaped to her feet, running toward us.

A microsecond after my bullet hit Gold, Bob's heavy

.45 slug slammed into Duvon's chest. He was wearing a vest; I saw the puff of dust as the hollow point slug hit. It picked him up off his feet and hurled him backward. His head hit the concrete floor with a sickening crack.

"Stop, you bitch," Tree yelled and there was a burst of suppressed automatic fire: the slugs kicked up shards of concrete around Jacque's feet as she ran, and she stopped.

"Now back up... back up, back up, back up. That's it, now stop. Siddown and don't even twitch. You do, an' I'll turn your goddamn face into a goddamn milkshake."

She sat down.

Oh my God, I thought. *We've blown it.*

"Starke, you piece of garbage. You see that green dot on her face? That's me. I'm gonna kill you, man, and your goddamn buddy, but I'm gonna make you suffer first. I'm gonna blow your knees an' elbows away, and then I'm gonna gut shoot you both. You know how a .223 works, don't you, Starke? It hits an' then it starts a spinnin'. One in the gut an' it'll turn your innards into mush. It'll take an hour for you to die."

I still couldn't see him. I could see the dot wavering over Jacque's face, though. And I could tell by his voice that he was close to losing it.

"Okay, Shady," I shouted. "We're coming out. Don't shoot her."

"Harry," Bob hissed. "We go out there, we're dead. We won't make it three feet."

"I don't think so. I think he wants to hurt us first. We have to hope Kate can do something before he does." I looked east to see if I could see her; I couldn't. "Here goes nothing."

"Harry, you can't save her. He's gonna kill her no matter what we do."

"Not if I can help it."

I dropped my two VPs on the concrete and stepped around the doorframe and into view.

I didn't get the chance to take another step. A hail of automatic fire skittered off the concrete around my feet, and I stopped dead.

He laughed. "Scared you, huh? Now your buddy. Step out, Bob. Do it now, or Harry dies on the spot." Bob stepped out and dropped his weapons.

"Now then. That's a whole lot better. Walk forward —slowly, slowly! Go to the chairs and sit down with your little friend. Do it *now*!"

And then I could see him, and he wasn't alone. Up on the catwalk, close to the stairs, Tree had an M-16 at his right shoulder and Jonathan Greene at his left. The greasy little son of a bitch was grinning... no he was *snarling* down at us. Even at that distance I could see his right wrist was in a cast.

"I said *sit down*, Starke!" Tree loosed another burst of fire at my feet. We sat, and watched as they descended the iron stairs together. I looked at Duvon. He was ten feet or so away, still on his back, still unconscious.

Where the hell is Kate?

"Well, Harry," Tree said as they approached. The M-16 was now tucked comfortably under his right arm, but his finger was on the trigger and the muzzle never wavered from my chest.

"You sure as hell screwed up our little operation. Well, it wasn't so little, was it, John Boy?" Tree glanced sideways at Greene. "Oh well, it's no biggy. We still have the product, and the men we can replace. But you two? Well now.... Oh, and how's your sexy blond girlfriend? You can be sure I'll pay her a little visit when we're done here. I know where you live. How the hell you made my guys the other night.... Ah, never mind. As I was saying, I'll pay your girl a little visit an' screw her seven ways to Christmas before I cut her throat."

He paused, looked down at me. Maybe he was hoping for some sort of reaction. He didn't get one.

"Cat got your tongue, Harry? Oh, now there's a thought. Maybe I should start with your tongue. You don't talk nothin' but a load o' shit with it anyway." He hefted the M-16 still under his arm. "So, where to begin...."

"For God's sake, stop screwing around and finish him," Greene snarled. "If you don't want to do it, I will."

"Patience, Johnny Boy. All in good time. I've waited a lot of years for this. Remember this, Harry?"

He showed me his left forearm. The dimpled scar on his wrist glowed white in the dim light. It was the result of a bullet I'd put in him a several years ago when I was working the Robinson case.

"I told you I'd make you pay for it, didn't I?" He looked at Greene. "Better tie 'em up, Johnny. See to it, will you?"

"Who the hell do you think you're ordering around you stupid son of a bitch. Do you have any idea what this mess has cost us? You tie him up. Better yet, kill them all, and let's get the hell out of here."

"Tsk, tsk, tsk," Tree murmured, looking first at Bob, then at me. "So ungrateful. Do you have these problems with your employees, Harry?"

"*Employees?*" Greene screeched. "You work for *me* you crazy bastard. Gimme that gun. I'll do it."

"Now hold awn there, Trigger. We got business to conduct first, me an' ol' Harry heah." I almost laughed; the impersonation of Pat Buttram's Sherriff of Nottingham in Disney's *Robin Hood* was almost perfect.

Greene did not appreciate it, however. He turned away, walked to the where Bob had dropped his 1911s, grabbed one off the floor, racked the slide, and came back almost at the run, the gun held at arm's length pointing straight at me.

"No, no, no, no, no," Tree said lightly, and as Greene came barreling past him he slammed the barrel of the M-16 down on Greene's wrist. The 1911 flew out of his hand and skittered across the floor, much to my relief. "I told you to be patient, didn't I? Take it easy, you heah?"

Where the hell is Kate?

Then, as if in answer to a prayer: "Put the weapon down, Tree, slowly. Do not make any sudden moves, either of you." It was Kate. She stepped out of the shadows at the northeast corner of the room.

"Awe, Harry, you done lied to me," Tree said reasonably, shaking his head. "Now that wasn't nice."

"Better do as she says, Shady. You too, Johnny."

Carefully, Tree laid the M-16 down beside him.

"Kick it away," she said, and he did.

We stood up, all three of us. Bob cut the piece of rope that held Jacque's hands. She slumped against him and burst into tears.

"I'm sorry," Tree said. "Did I do that?" This time it was Urkle, and perfect. He truly was off his rocker.

"Turn around, you piece of crap," Bob growled. "You too, Greene." He ran his hands over their bodies, took a tiny .25 revolver from one of Tree's socks, tossed it across the room, then said, "Put your hands behind you, both of you. Stretch 'em out. Good." He looped a plastic tie over each one, jerked them tight, and then pushed them both toward the chairs.

"Ooh, nice and warm," Tree said, as he sat down on the chair Jacque had just vacated. "Can't stand a cold seat, can you?"

Bob didn't answer. He just walked around back of Greene, put one hand under his chin, the other on top of his head, and with a quick, sickening jerk, broke his neck. The loud crack it made almost turned my stomach.

I stared, suddenly cold, as Bob let go of him and Greene toppled slowly forward, out of the chair and onto his knees on the floor. He kept going until his face hit the floor, and there he remained as if prayer, facing Mecca. He was gone.

For a moment there was dead silence, and then: "*What the f....* Christ Almighty, Bob." I said it almost in a whisper.," I was stunned.

Kate screeched, "Bob! You... you *killed* him!"

"Yep, head of the snake, remember? And here goes another," Bob growled as he stepped sideways, behind Shady. Before he could touch him, however, a voice screamed down at us from the catwalk.

"You bastards! You filthy pieces of shit!"

It was a woman's voice, and no sooner was the last word out of her mouth than something akin to a sledgehammer hit me in the center of my back, and then another high on my left shoulder. *Bam. Bam.*

And then I was going down, pitching forward, twisting, clawing for the Smith and Wesson M&P Shield in my ankle holster. As I fell I looked up, and there she was: Kathryn Greene. She was standing on the walkway, her face twisted with rage, a pistol in her right hand aimed straight at me.

She fired again. The slug hit the plate on the right side, half sleeve of my body armor. I hit the floor on my back. By instinct, I swung the Shield upward and fired once, one-handed. The slug hit her upper left arm, spinning her around, blood spraying out over the rail, but she wasn't done yet. Screaming like a demon, she continued the spin, righted herself, and came back into firing position, her left arm hanging loose at her side. She fired again. I felt the slug tear through the soft, fatty tissue of the inside of my lower left arm.

Jesus Christ!

I fired back instinctively; there was no time to aim. I hit her low in the right hip, and she staggered back, gun still raised, but before she could fire again I got off two more shots. The first missed; the second didn't. It hit her in the mouth. Her head snapped back, her eyes wide; her hand dropped to her side and the gun slid from her already lifeless fingers. Slowly, she collapsed to her knees, then fell forward onto the catwalk, her hand hanging over the side, her fingers dripping blood. It all happened so quickly. No one else had even moved.

And then Kate was running toward me. "Jesus, Harry, are you okay?"

"Hell no," I gasped. I was flat on my back, the back of my head on the floor, pain surging through my body from the multiple hits to the body armor and the tear in my left arm. I couldn't even lift it to look at the damage.

"Oh shit," she whispered, kneeling beside me.

"What? *What?*"

She shook her head. "It's through and through."

"That's good, right?"

"Jeez," Bob said, leaning over her. "That ain't good. You need a hospital, and quick."

"What the hell?" I tried to roll over and get to my feet. I got only part way before I had to give it up and fall back. The pain was too bad. I did manage to get a look at the pool of blood, though, and Bob was right. It wasn't good.

"Bob," Kate said. "Gimme one of those cable ties, quickly."

She looped it around my upper arm and pulled it tight. The flow of blood stopped. It would work for a few minutes, but it would have to come off soon or I'd lose the arm.

"It's the exit wound," she said. "Bob's right. We need help, and quick."

She needn't have worried. It was already arriving. Church Street was turning into a circus. Someone must have heard the gunfire, probably the first responders at the fire station, and called it in.

Well at least they don't have far to come, I thought.

Within minutes the great windows were ablaze with flashing red and blue, amber, and white lights.

"Okay," I said. "Get ready. They'll come storming in here any minute. Hey…. We've got our story down, right?"

I laid my S&W down on the floor. "Bob, Jacque, stand still, keep your hands in sight at all times, don't move and for sure don't say a damned thing to anyone. "

"Where the hell is Shady?" Kate asked, looking around.

I tried to sit up. I made it onto my right elbow and looked around. The chair he'd been sitting in was empty. The cable tie was lying on the floor in front of it, the fastener broken. Not a difficult thing to do if you know how, and Shady obviously did.

From beyond the shadows, through the door under the catwalk, came the roar of a motorcycle engine. It was indeed, we found out later, the room where the overhead door was located, where I'd first spotted Tree relieving himself. The engine revved once. There was a screech of rubber on concrete, and then the sound of the engine slowly diminished as it raced away.

Son of a bitch. He's gone. He's gotten away.

But there was no time to dwell on that. The cops would be here any minute.

"Kate," I said through gritted teeth, trying to get her attention. She was still looking up toward where we'd heard the motorcycle. "You get on out there, quick. Identify yourself, try to explain why we're here and what we were doing. They come busting in, they could take us for the bad guys."

She nodded, and ran off into the shadows toward where the sounds of hammering could be heard. They were probably trying to break down the door.

I heard her shouting something. Then there was a loud crash as the door gave way, and then.... Chaos? Yeah, that was probably the right word. The first people to enter the building were the Cleveland police chief, Bobby Masterson, and Lucas Jackson, one of his captains. Both had weapons in their hands. Kate was between them.

Fortunately, I knew both of them, and even better, they both knew me.

"Well," Masterson said, coming to stand over me as he holstered his pistol, "it had to happen sooner or later, I suppose."

"What did?" I asked. "And hello to you too, Bobby."

"I figured you'd find a way to invade my patch, and it looks like you did. Did you get 'em?"

"Er... get who?"

"Come on, Harry. Don't play cute with me. You're not on the golf course now and, by the look of that arm, you won't be for quite a while. Did you get Tree and his mob?"

"You knew about them?"

"You think we're country boys here in Cleveland? Don't know our asses from our elbows? Of course we knew about them. We've been watching them for months, at least Lucas here has. Never was able to find any cause to enter the property. The owner"—he looked at what was left of Kathryn Greene up on the catwalk—"she and her shyster husband wouldn't allow access, not without a warrant.... Well, you know all about that, don't you, Harry. Never did believe in warrants, did you. And here you are, and what a damned mess you've made for us to clean up." He grinned down at me. "And I thank you for it."

"Oh, you're welcome," I said dryly. And then I introduced the others.

"Yeah," he said. "I know Bob Ryan, and the lieutenant. We've run into each other in the past. How are you, Catherine?" he nodded in her direction. "Ms. Hale though, I didn't know. But now I do." He sighed at me, and shook his head....." He cast a glance at her, then turned again to me.

"Women, Harry? You brought women to a gunfight? What the hell were you thinking?"

I didn't answer.

"You should have called me, Harry. You know that, right?"

I nodded.

"Then why didn't you?"

I simply shrugged, and immediately regretted it as spears of agony shot up my arm.

"Hang in there," he said. "The paramedics are their way. Oh, and so is the DA, and the TBI. I had to call 'em in. No choice. Besides, our crime scene unit isn't big enough to handle this place." He looked around, shaking his head. "How many, Harry?"

"How many what?

"How many did you kill?" He looked at the still-unconscious Duvon James. "He dead?"

"I don't think so. There are only... three dead, I think. Gold over there. Her up the catwalk... and him." I nodded in Jonathan Greene's direction.

"There are some wounded," I continued, "and some people tied up all over the building.... Look, Bobby. I don't want to lose this arm. I need medical attention."

"They're coming. Should be here in a couple of minutes. In the meantime, why don't you tell me what the hell happened to him," the chief said, looking down at Greene.

I looked at Kate; Kate looked at Bob; we all kept our mouths shut.

"Looks like an accident to me," Jackson said, his face perfectly blank.

"Accident?" Masterson raised an eyebrow. "How the hell can it be an accident? He's kneeling with his face on the floor and his hands tied behind his back with a cable tie, for Christ's sake."

"No he isn't. He's over there at the bottom of the

stairs. Must have gotten excited, slipped, and... fell?" He screwed up his face quizzically as he said it.

Masterson looked sideways at him, a skeptical look on his face. He was shaking his head, grimly, then his attitude seemed to change. He smiled down at me, then said forcefully, "Yeah, that's it, an accident. Captain Jackson, you got a minute?" He was talking to Jackson, but he was looking at me. "Just a couple of minutes," he continued. "You and I, we need to go get the boys organized. We need to begin clearing the building, and getting the paramedics in here. You folks hang tight," he told us. "Don't touch anything. Don't move anything. Help will be here in a minute."

He took hold of Jackson's arm, turned him around, and steered him toward the shadows.

Once they'd disappeared, Bob took a quick step forward, grabbed the lifeless Greene around the waist, and carried him easily to the foot of the stairs. He dropped him hard on the bottom step. I cringed as the back of his neck hit the edge of the steel tread. He took out a small pocketknife, sliced through the plastic tie, stuffed the tie and the knife back into his pocket, took a step back, stepped forward again and rearranged Greene's arms, then stepped back again and surveyed his handiwork.

"That should fix it," he said. "He wasn't tied long enough, or tight enough, to make ligature marks." And then he walked quickly back and knelt down beside Kate, who was cutting the cable tie around my arm. He made it with not a moment to spare.

At least a dozen of Cleveland's finest came boiling in out of the shadows, along with a half dozen paramedics. They were quickly followed by Masterson and Jackson, who were accompanied by a tall man wearing jeans and a golf shirt. I could tell just by his attitude that the third man was the DA.

He questioned me at length while the paramedics readied me for the hospital. He listened skeptically to everything I had to say—I made sure that Kate, Bob, and Jacque did too—and then he turned to Masterson.

"You believe any of that bullshit?" he asked him.

"Yeah, Dell. I believe it. How the hell we would have jerked that mob outa here if not for Starke and his crew, I don't know. The Greenes had the place battened down tight. No one ever saw Tree. I, for one, am grateful. We all should be."

I couldn't believe what I was hearing. Here we were, surrounded by bodies and wounded, and they were... grateful. They were taking no action. Yeah right. Been there, done that. There ain't nothing that easy, and while maybe Bobby could handle the DA, I knew I still had the TBI to cope with.

Ten minutes later I was on the way to the Skyridge hospital emergency room. They hauled me into triage, then straight to the OR. Yep, it was a bad one. I was lucky not to lose my arm. The nine-millimeter full metal jacket slug had ploughed a hole through my arm. The exit wound.... Well, I'd seen a few of those in the past, and I'd been shot before, but this was different. Just to look at it scared the hell out of me, but that wasn't all. The slug had clipped the bone, carved a notch into it. The good news was I could wiggle all of my fingers and I had feeling in the fingertips, so by some miracle the tendons and nerves were still intact. The bad news: the slug had also severed an artery, and that required a stent. Masterson was right; I wouldn't be playing golf for quite a while. Still, bad as it was, it wasn't enough to keep me in the hospital more than two or three hours, just as long as it took to x-ray and repair the wound and the artery, and bandage it. When it was done I discharged myself, much to the dismay of the attending nurses and physicians, called Chief Masterson, and he had a cruiser pick me up. It was just after five in the morning.

20

Friday Morning, Early

The next six hours didn't exactly fly by either. We were kept separate from one another, which was standard practice, and they'd hauled Bob's Jeep into the compound, collected all of our weapons, and laid them out on the conference room table. There they garnered more than a few admiring looks, especially the suppressed Tavors.

"You went in there to kill, didn't you Harry?" Masterson said, hefting one of the rifles thoughtfully.

That one I was able to answer honestly. "No, Bobby, I didn't. I went in there prepared to kill if I had to, but I promised my father that we wouldn't, not unless it was absolutely unavoidable. Why do you think we carried the ties? You found the prisoners, right?"

He nodded. "That we did. Five of them. And four dead and nine wounded, two of whom are in critical condition. Jesus, Harry. That was a war you guys just fought. You're lucky you all are still alive, and mostly unhurt. I'm not even going to ask you what happened to that slimy little bastard Greene...."

He was interrupted when the door to conference room opened and two people I knew well walked in: Special Agents Gordon Caster and Sergio Mendez of the Tennessee Bureau Of Investigation. Both of whom I'd had dealings with only a few months earlier.

"I knew it," Caster said, dropping down into one of plush seats on the other side of the big table. "Sooner or later, I knew we'd run into you again. How's Kate, by the way?"

I grinned at him. "She's fine. She's downstairs somewhere. I'm sure you'll get to see her."

"Oh yeah, you can be sure of that."

"Were you in on this raid, Chief?" Caster asked.

Bobby didn't hesitate. "We were."

I couldn't believe what I was hearing.

"What about Gazzara? Why was a Chattanooga PD homicide detective involved?"

Oh hell, here we go, I thought. *Now the crap will hit the fan.*

But I was wrong. Chief Bobby must have been in touch with Chief Johnston in Chattanooga, because what he said next just about bowled me over.

"It was a mutual aid operation. We've had the Greenes under observation for more than three months. Since they were operating out of Chattanooga I asked Chief Johnston for aid. Lieutenant Gazzara was detached and placed on loan to us. Johnston also recommended we involve Mr. Starke. Apparently he knows the Greene's and Lester Tree quite well, is that not so, Mr. Starke?"

Caster grinned at him. I could tell it was all he could do not to burst out laughing.

"Bobby," he said. "You are so full of crap you could fertilize a half dozen acres of corn. You think you're fooling anyone? I know exactly what happed here, and so do you. Starke here found out that Tree murdered his brother and he came after him. It's that simple."

Masterson stared stoically at him, his mouth clamped shut, his lips flat.

"No comment, Bobby? Can't say as I blame you, but no worries, Golden Boy here gets another free pass. We did, after all, get a lot of bad guys off the streets, not to mention the haul. That being said, Harry, we still have a few details to clear up before you and your army of three can be on your way home."

And so it went on. It was tough, but for the most part they were respectful, and by the time they were done I knew that Bobby Masterson had not been joking when he'd thanked me earlier, back at the Old Woolen Mill.

The Cleveland PD, the District Attorney, and of course the TBI would take credit for the raid, for shutting down the drug ring, and for the bust, and it was a big one. They found seventeen hundred pounds of marijuana packed in one-pound packages, twenty kilos of high-grade coke ready to cut, and they were still counting the pills when we left at eleven thirty that morning. Oh, and then of course there was the $447,000 in cash. Yep, it was a big bust.

My team's part in it would, for a change, be kept quiet. No media, no hassle, and best of all, no charges. And... no guns. They kept the whole damned lot, including the vests.

Kate, Chief Johnston, and the Chattanooga PD, however, would get the recognition and credit they deserved for their part in the mutual aid operation.

So all in all, everyone was happy except me. Shady Tree was still missing.

When we finally got out of there it was close to lunchtime, and I was starving. Not only that, my arm was throbbing with pain like I'd never known. I'd been given some painkillers, Percocet, at the hospital, but they weren't for me; I needed some Ibuprofen, something to drink, and some food—in that order.

I'd called Amanda almost as soon as I got out of the hospital. No, I didn't tell her any of what had happened. I was in no mood, and I sure as hell didn't tell her about my wound. She did, however, agree to come and get us—Bob's Jeep was still in the compound, and was likely to stay there for a while, and she was waiting for us in the Cleveland PD lobby when they finally turned us loose. As always, she looked amazing, and it was only then that I realized what a sorry-looking bunch we must have been.

Be that as it may, she took one look at me and she flipped out. It took me a good five minutes to reassure her that I was all right, that the wound to my arm, though easily the worst I'd ever received, would heal and that I would eventually regain full use of it.

She didn't like that word "eventually," and, to be truthful, neither did I, but that's what the surgeon who patched me up said, so I had to believe it.

During the ride back home—yes, all of us got to leave then, including Jacque—Amanda was quiet. I asked her what was wrong, several times, but all she would say was, "Nothing, Harry."

21

Friday Afternoon

We arrived at the house to find August and Rose waiting for us. We climbed out of the car, and Rose took one look at my arm in its sling and did that that thing Macaulay Culkin did in Home Alone. Then she grabbed me, flung her arms around my neck, and squeezed. I was quite touched.

My old man? He just stood by, shaking his head until Rose let me loose.

"You okay, son?" he asked.

Before I could answer, Amanda turned and walked quickly into the house. She said not a word, nor did she look back; she simply disappeared.

Jeez, what the hell's up with her?

I spent the next five minutes giving August and Rose the short version—the details I saved for later—and then I went looking for her. I found her in the bedroom, flat on her face, on the bed. I thought she was crying; she wasn't; she was as mad as hell.

I went and sat down beside her, put my hand on her shoulder. "Hey. What's wrong?"

She shrugged away my hand, rolled over, and then sat up. Boy was she angry.

"Damn you, Harry Starke. How can you ask such a stupid question? What the hell d'you think is wrong? Look at you. You look like hell, and so do the others, but at least they all managed to come back in one piece, but not you, oh hell no. Every time you walk out of here you come back banged up all to hell."

"Honey, that's not—"

"Harry, shut your mouth for once and let me speak. You're lucky you didn't lose your arm. And *this!*" She grabbed the sleeve of my T-shirt and jerked it up over my shoulder, revealing the ugly black bruise where Kathryn Greene's bullet had slammed into my body armor. "How many more times were you hit?"

I opened my mouth to speak, but she interrupted me.

"No, show me! Show me your back. *Now!*"

Reluctantly, I let her pull the T-shirt over my head, and I heard her sharp intake of breath when she saw it.

"Oh my God. I knew it. You couldn't sit still in the car. You had to lean forward the whole way home. Have you seen it?"

I shook my head.

"Go look at it. Go on."

I shrugged and went to the bathroom, the T-shirt hanging over the sling.

It did look pretty bad, but they were only bruises, and I'd seen worse. They'd actually look a whole lot worse later on. I went back to her. I was smiling, but then I saw the look on her face. It was... well, you had to see it.

"C'mere," she said quietly. "Sit down." She had a pot of Blue Emu in her hand.

She spent the next five minutes rubbing the stuff into my bruises. She didn't say a word to me the whole time. Finally, she screwed the top on the pot, put it down on the nightstand, and lay back on the pillows, staring up at me.

"Thank you," I said, and leaned over her, intending to kiss her. She put both hands flat on my chest and pushed me away.

"Hey!" I said.

"That's not going to get it, Harry. A kiss is not good enough. You seem to think that will fix anything—not anymore. But it's not even that. You and me... we can't go on like this. One of these days you're going to come home in a box.... No. Stop it! Get away from me." Again she pushed me away.

"I mean it, Harry. You'll be forty-six next year and you're still acting and thinking like Wild Bill Hickok, and it's going to get you killed."

"She's right, Harry."

I looked up. My father was standing in the open doorway.

"She's right," he repeated. "Listen to her." And then he turned and walked away. I got up and closed the door after him.

"So what are you saying?" I asked, sitting back down beside her.

"I don't know. I just don't know. I know you, Harry. I know what you are, and I know you can't change, so...."

"Wait. Are you saying what I think you're saying? You want to call off the wedding?"

She shook her head. "No, that's not what I'm saying. But I do want you to stop acting like—like one of the damned X-men. For God's sake, Harry, we have a police force to do what you do. You don't have to take the risks you do. Let them do it. It's what they get paid for."

"You want me to quit my work, what I do for a living?" I asked quietly.

"I want you to stop taking unnecessary risks! I don't want to wake up one morning and find you gone forever!"

"Okay," I said. "You got it."

She looked at me, wide-eyed. "Just like that?"

"Just like that."

"You promise?"

"I promise."

I could tell she didn't believe me for a second—but then she did. "Oh, Harry." She flung her arms around my neck and squeezed.

Yep, I said it and, at the time, I meant it. It wasn't long after, though, that I realized it wasn't something I should have said. I never go looking for this stuff; it comes looking for me. Still, I'd made her a promise and I was going to do my best to keep it. I didn't want to lose her either.

22

Friday Evening

Jacque gathered her belongings and went home to Wendy. Kate and Bob did the same. Well, they went off together. That left me and Amanda with Rose and August.

The weather had turned, the sun was shining, and all was right with the world. I called Dinner Delivered—no one wanted to cook, least of all me—and ordered for delivery around seven o'clock, and by three that afternoon we were out by the pool. August and Rose and I were seated at a table under an umbrella with a Yeti cooler full of ice, gin, Laphroaig, and several bottles of white wine. We watched Amanda swimming laps: long, slow strokes that propelled her through the water like a miniature torpedo.

Finally she climbed the steps out of the water, grabbed a towel, and proceeded to dry her hair. She was wearing a white bikini, her body glistening in the sunshine, the drops of water sparkling as they ran down her belly. *Damn, she's beautiful.*

Eventually the show was over, and she joined us at the table. She noted that my glass was empty, and, knowing I couldn't do it myself—the arm had stiffened drastically and I could barely move it—she poured me a fresh drink, leaned over and kissed me, and then poured a glass of wine for herself.

The view from the patio that afternoon and evening was stunning. By eight o'clock it was twilight, and the lights of the city had turned it into a glittering net of jewels.

Me? I was in a somewhat pensive mood, thinking about my life, my family, my friends, and my brother, Henry. And I daydreamed. It was one of those rare moments when I was truly at peace with myself and the world.

"Harry. Wake up." It was August that jerked me out of my reverie.

I turned and smiled at him. "Hey."

"Well, are you going to tell us?" he asked.

I didn't want to, but I did. I told them the whole story, from parking Bob's Jeep under the tree to calling Amanda to come and fetch us, and the three of them listened in silence until I'd finished. The only thing I left out was Bob breaking Greene's neck. I didn't tell them how he died, just that he had. And I wondered if I'd pay for that omission one day, and for the deaths of Henry Gold and Kathryn Greene. Tree was out there somewhere, and like a bad penny he was sure to turn up again. And then there was the congressman. He would never forgive me for killing his daughter.

I shook the thoughts out of my head. And I surely didn't mention them to Amanda and my father.

"I kept my word, Dad. I tried my best not to kill, but...."

He nodded slowly, his eyes on mine. "I know you did, son.... So Tree got away?"

"He did. He was the only one. They got everyone else."

"Is he the one who killed Henry?"

"He was responsible, but no, he didn't kill him. That was Duvon James. He won't be charged, though. Other than what Tree said, there's no proof, no evidence."

August shook his head sadly. Rose put a hand on his arm.

"Don't, Dad," I said. "He'll do his time. A lot of time. In fact, he'll probably spend the rest of his days in a prison hospital. The surgeon who patched me up told me that he fractured his skull when he hit the concrete floor. He's in a coma, and even if he comes out of it there's a real chance he'll have brain damage. If he does come out of it, and if he's still sentient, they'll have him on a whole litany of drug charges. He'll get his."

And we talked on into the night until I was almost falling off my chair. No, I wasn't drunk. Far from it. I was drained, exhausted. It was almost midnight.

I was so tired Amanda had to lead me off, and then help me with my clothes. I lay down in bed beside her.

The night was cool, the windows were open; she smelled wonderful, and that was... all I remember.

The End

This book, *Retribution*, is Book 7 in the Harry Starke series. If you enjoyed it, you may also enjoy reading *Calypso*, Book 8. To get a copy CLICK HERE or simply cut and paste this URL: https://readerlinks.com/l/182933

ACKNOWLEDGMENTS

There are several people I'd like to thank for their help during the creation of this book.

Thank you Dr. Ron Coleman of Cleveland for allowing me access to your beautiful old and iconic building, and for allowing me to feature it in the story. Dr. Coleman purchased the Old Woolen Mill I used as a principle character in the story in 1999, and has since developed a unique vision for the complex. Way to go, Dr. Ron.

I would also like to thank Cleveland Police Chief Mark Gibson and Police Captain Robert Harbison for taking the time to talk to me, for their patience, and for their invaluable help and advice.

I would also like to thank all of my retired ex-cop friends for their help and insight, especially Ron Akers for his support, generosity, and expertise in firearms, and ex-Chattanooga homicide Detective Lieutenant Richard Heck for patiently answering my questions. Google Detective Richard Heck. I think you'll get a surprise.

My friend Jack Knapp: thank you for your unwavering support.

Finally, I'd like to thank my wife, Jo, for putting up

with my quirkiness during the writing process. Honey, I know I ain't easy to live with when I'm spending so much time with Harry and his friends. I love you.

MORE

Thank you.

Thank you for taking the time to read *Retribution*. If you enjoyed it, please consider telling your friends or posting a short review on Amazon (just a sentence will do). Word of mouth is an author's best friend, and much appreciated. Thank you. —Blair Howard.

Reviews are so very important. I don't have the backing of a major New York publisher, and I can't afford take out ads in the newspapers or on TV, but you can help get the word out.

To those many of my readers who have already posted reviews to this and my other novels, thank you for your past and continued support.

If you have comments or questions, you can contact me by e-mail at blair@blairhoward.com, and you can visit my website http://www.blairhoward.com.

Made in the USA
Monee, IL
22 June 2022